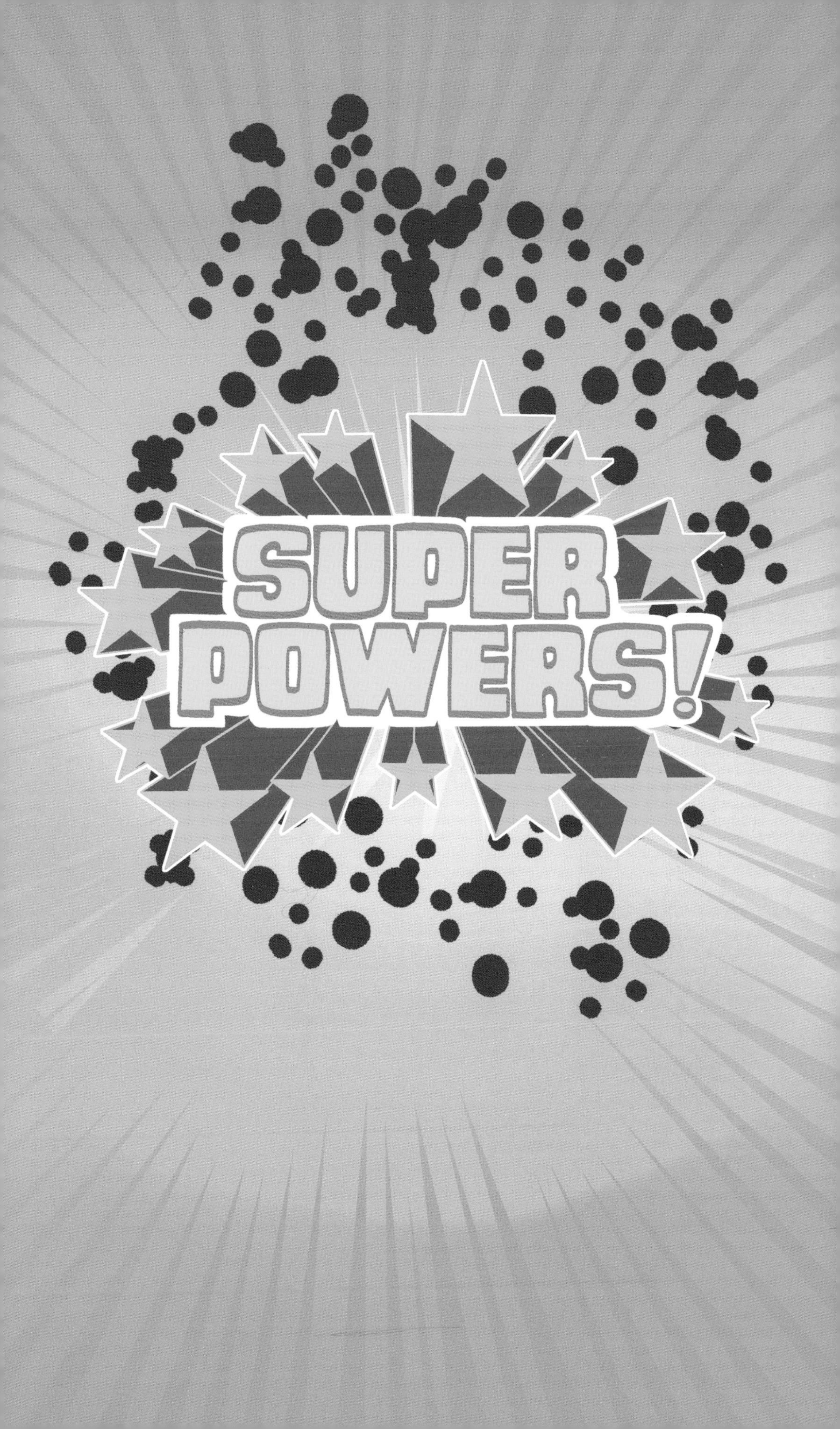
SUPER
POWERS!

Super Powers! is published by
Stone Arch Books,
A Capstone Imprint
1710 Roe Crest Drive
North Mankato, Minnesota 56003
www.mycapstone.com

Cataloging-in-Publication Data is available at the Library of Congress website:
ISBN: 978-1-4965-7396-4 (library binding)
ISBN 978-1-4965-7402-2 (eBook PDF)

Summary: Superman is hurt! While he heals in the Fortress of Solitude, Batman and the Flash face a villain from the future who's set his evil sights on "the Kryptonian."

Printed in the United States.
PA021

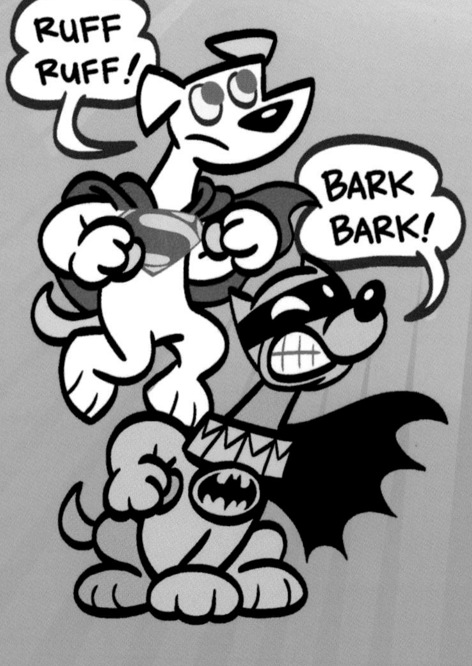
RUFF RUFF!
BARK BARK!

STONE ARCH BOOKS
Chris Harbo Editorial Director
Gena Chester Editor
Hilary Wacholz Art Director
Kris Wilfahrt Production Specialist

Superman created by Jerry Siegel and Joe Shuster. By special arrangement with the Jerry Siegel family.

Composite Crisis!

BY ART BALTAZAR AND FRANCO

STONE ARCH BOOKS
a capstone imprint

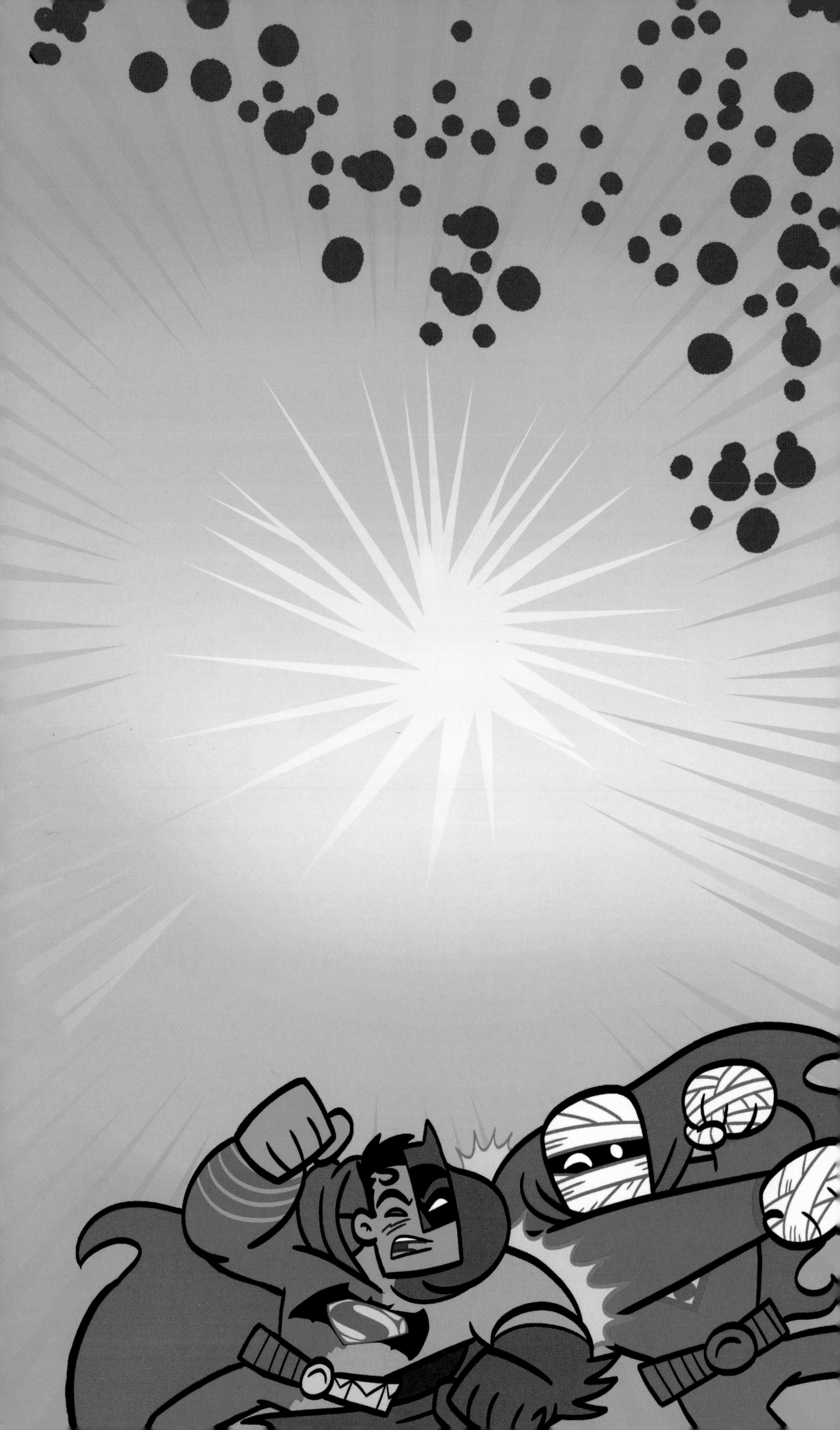

MEANWHILE...

IN THE MIDDLE OF THE PACIFIC...

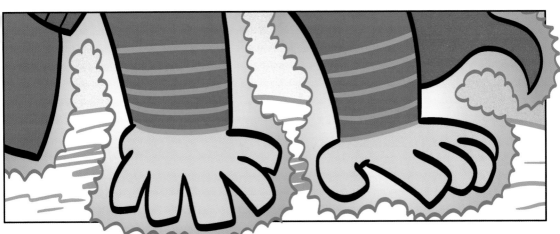

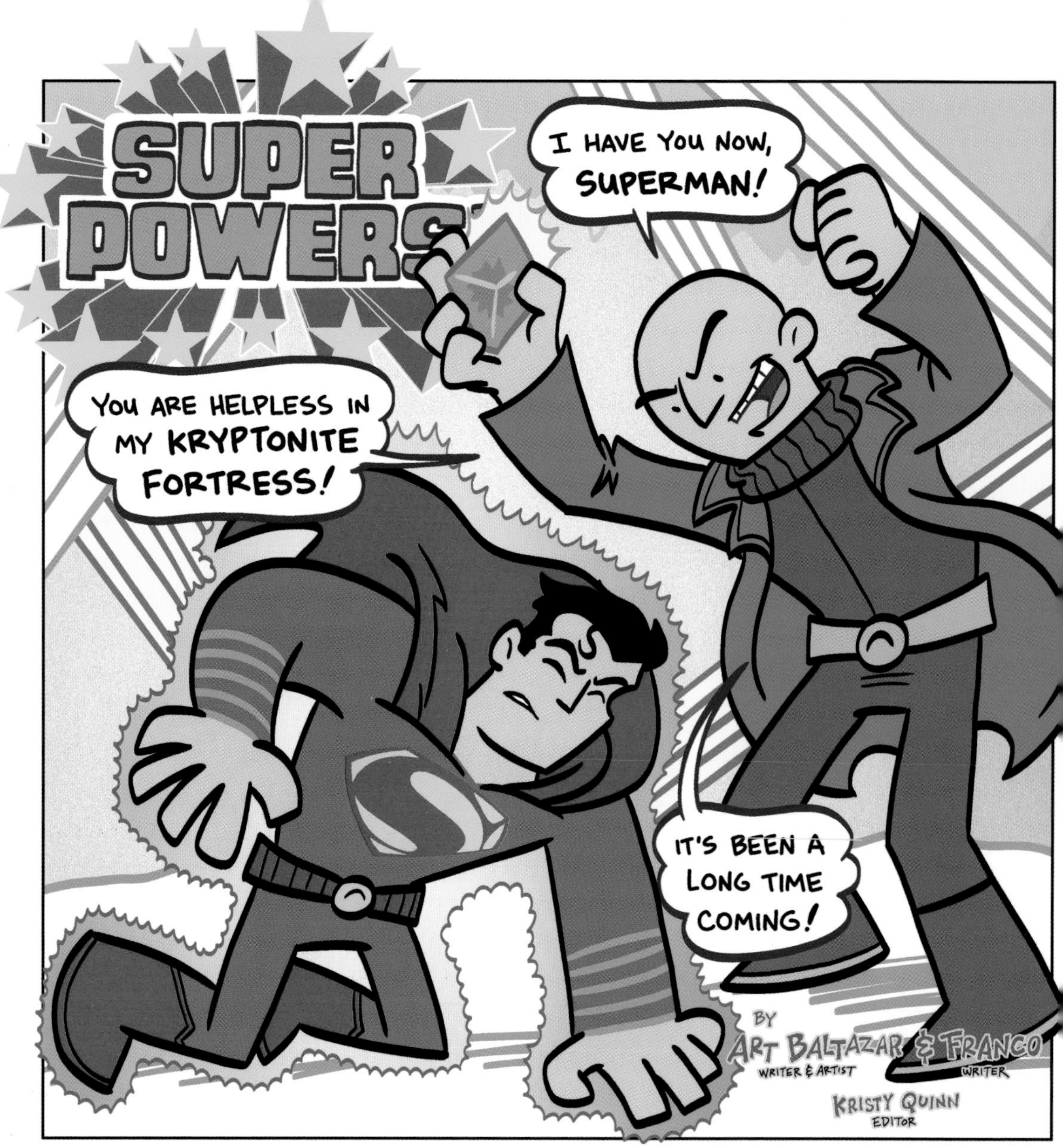
SUPER POWERS!
I HAVE YOU NOW, SUPERMAN!
YOU ARE HELPLESS IN MY KRYPTONITE FORTRESS!
IT'S BEEN A LONG TIME COMING!
BY
ART BALTAZAR
WRITER & ARTIST
& FRANCO
WRITER
KRISTY QUINN
EDITOR

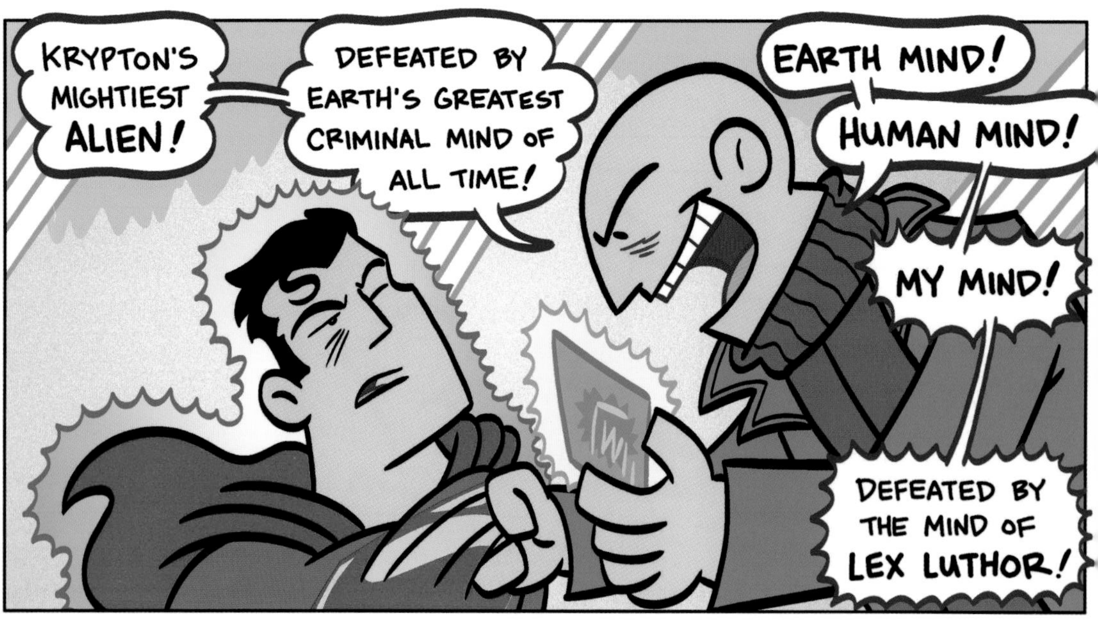
KRYPTON'S MIGHTIEST ALIEN!
DEFEATED BY EARTH'S GREATEST CRIMINAL MIND OF ALL TIME!
EARTH MIND!
HUMAN MIND!
MY MIND!
DEFEATED BY THE MIND OF LEX LUTHOR!

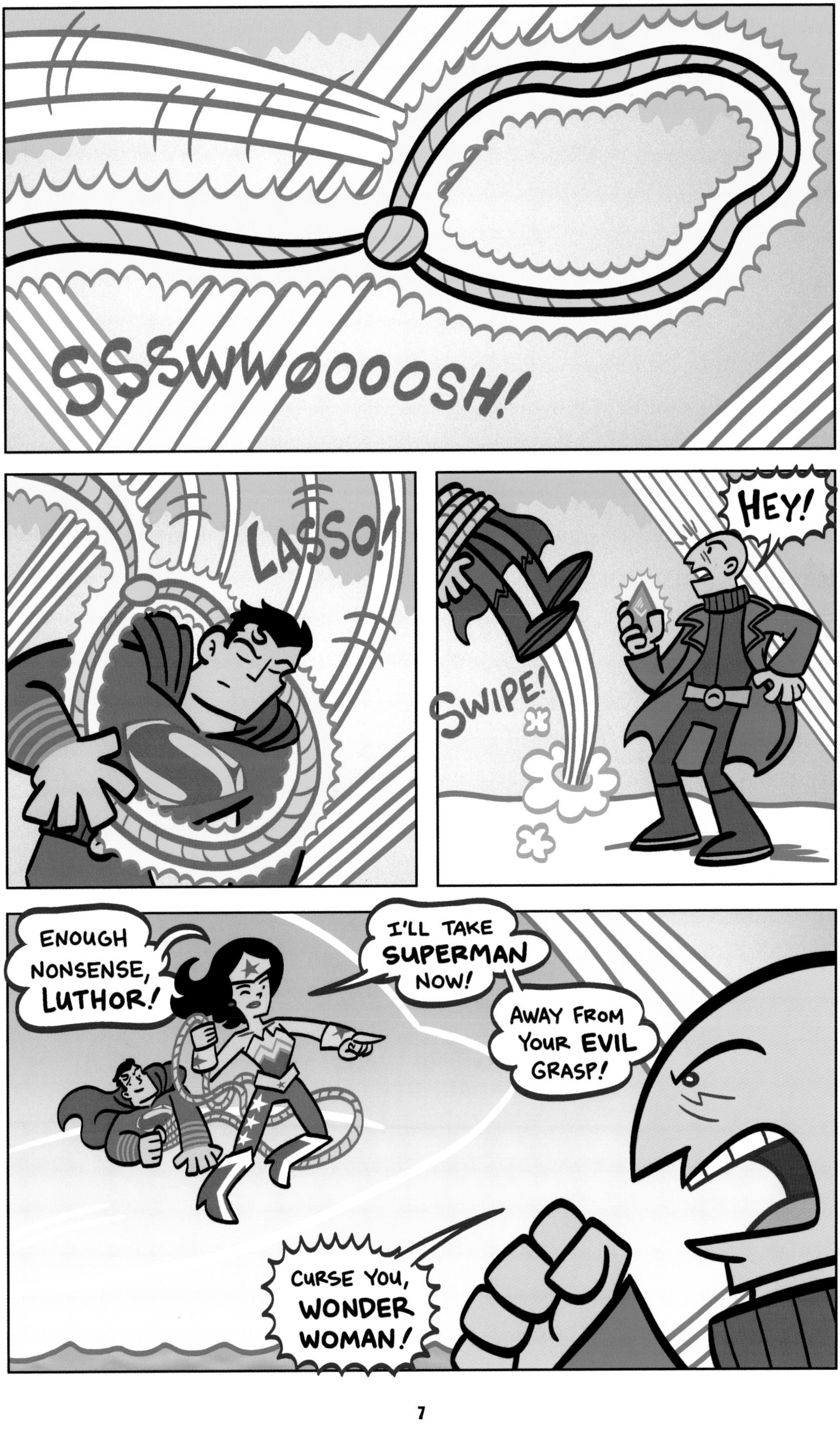
SSSWWØOOOOSH!
LASSO!
HEY!
SWIPE!
ENOUGH NONSENSE, LUTHOR!
I'LL TAKE SUPERMAN NOW!
AWAY FROM YOUR EVIL GRASP!
CURSE YOU, WONDER WOMAN!

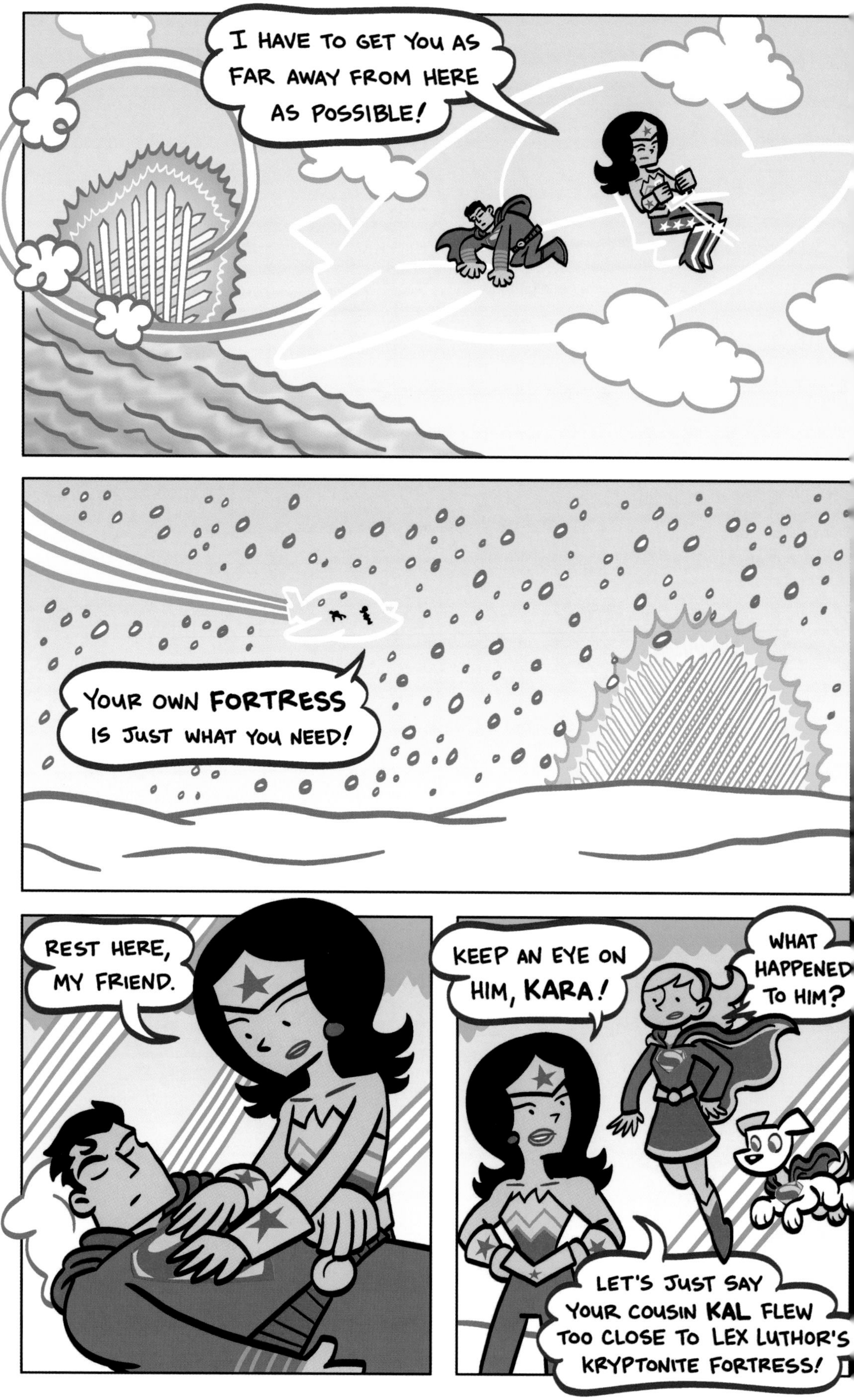

I HAVE TO GET YOU AS FAR AWAY FROM HERE AS POSSIBLE!
YOUR OWN FORTRESS IS JUST WHAT YOU NEED!
REST HERE, MY FRIEND.
KEEP AN EYE ON HIM, KARA!
WHAT HAPPENED TO HIM?
LET'S JUST SAY YOUR COUSIN KAL FLEW TOO CLOSE TO LEX LUTHOR'S KRYPTONITE FORTRESS!

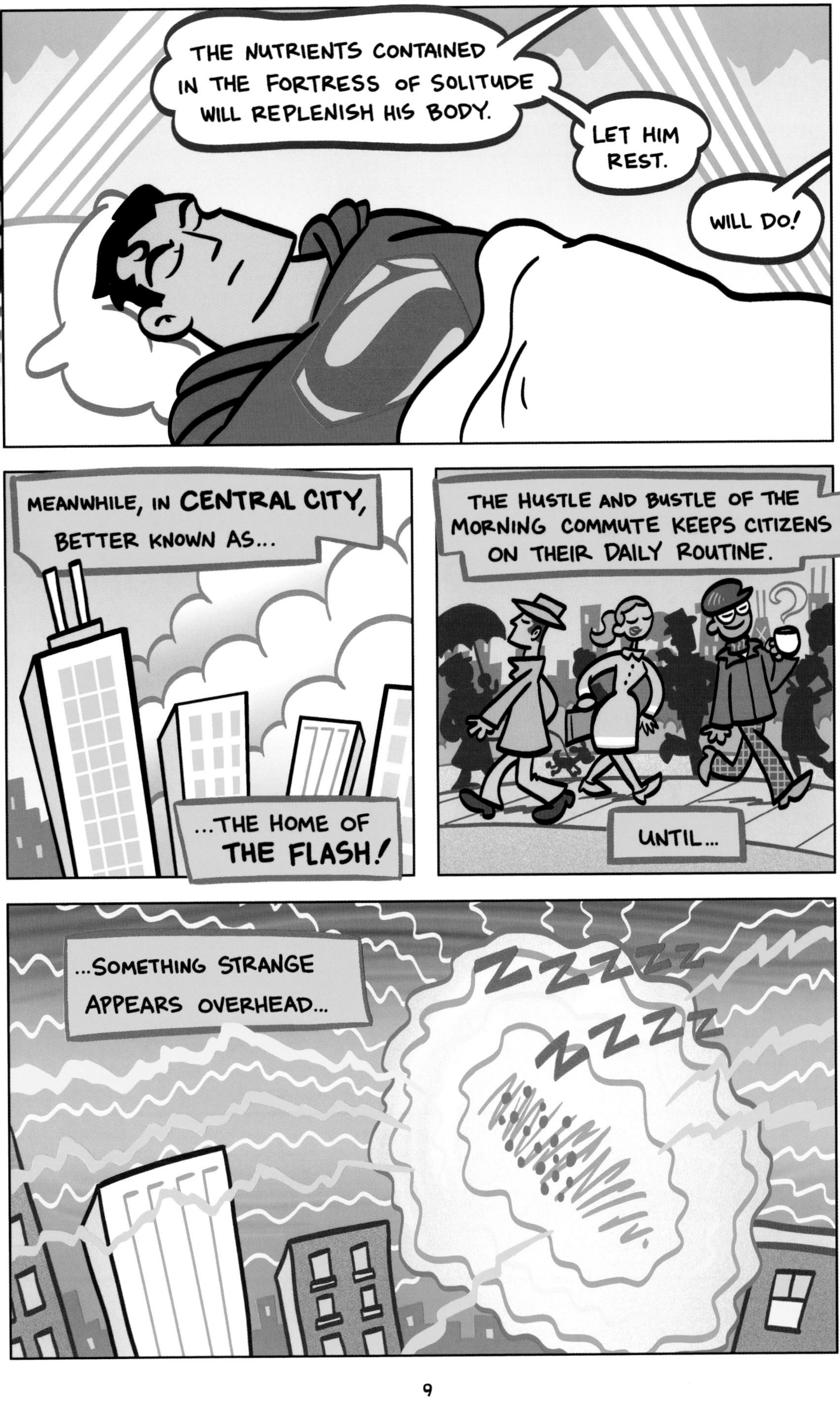
THE NUTRIENTS CONTAINED IN THE FORTRESS OF SOLITUDE WILL REPLENISH HIS BODY.
LET HIM REST.
WILL DO!
MEANWHILE, IN CENTRAL CITY, BETTER KNOWN AS...
...THE HOME OF THE FLASH!
THE HUSTLE AND BUSTLE OF THE MORNING COMMUTE KEEPS CITIZENS ON THEIR DAILY ROUTINE.
UNTIL...
...SOMETHING STRANGE APPEARS OVERHEAD...
ZZZZZ
ZZZZ

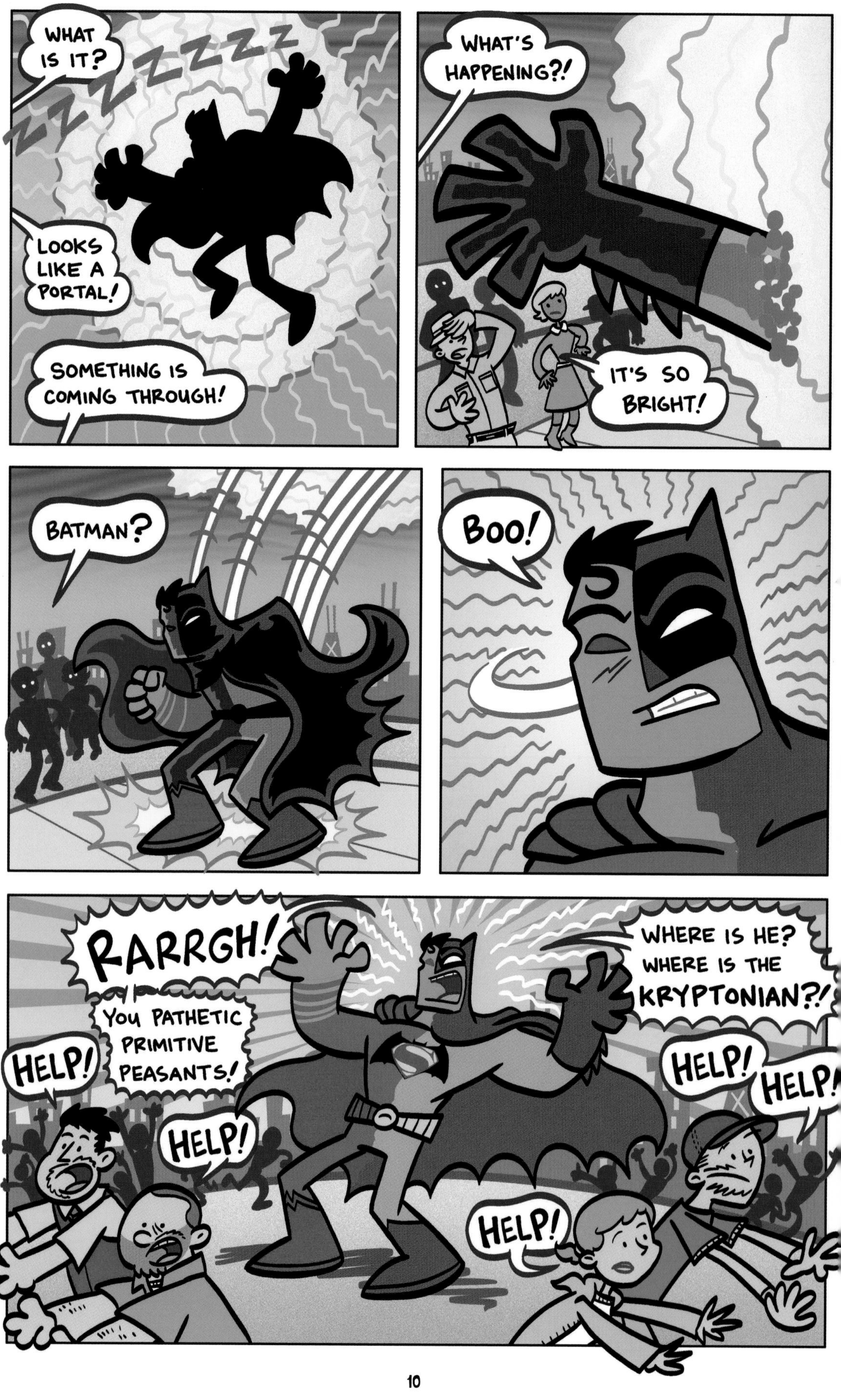
WHAT IS IT?
ZZZZZZZZ
LOOKS LIKE A PORTAL!
SOMETHING IS COMING THROUGH!
WHAT'S HAPPENING?!
IT'S SO BRIGHT!
BATMAN?
BOO!
RARRGH!
YOU PATHETIC PRIMITIVE PEASANTS!
WHERE IS HE? WHERE IS THE KRYPTONIAN?!
HELP!
HELP!
HELP!
HELP!
HELP!

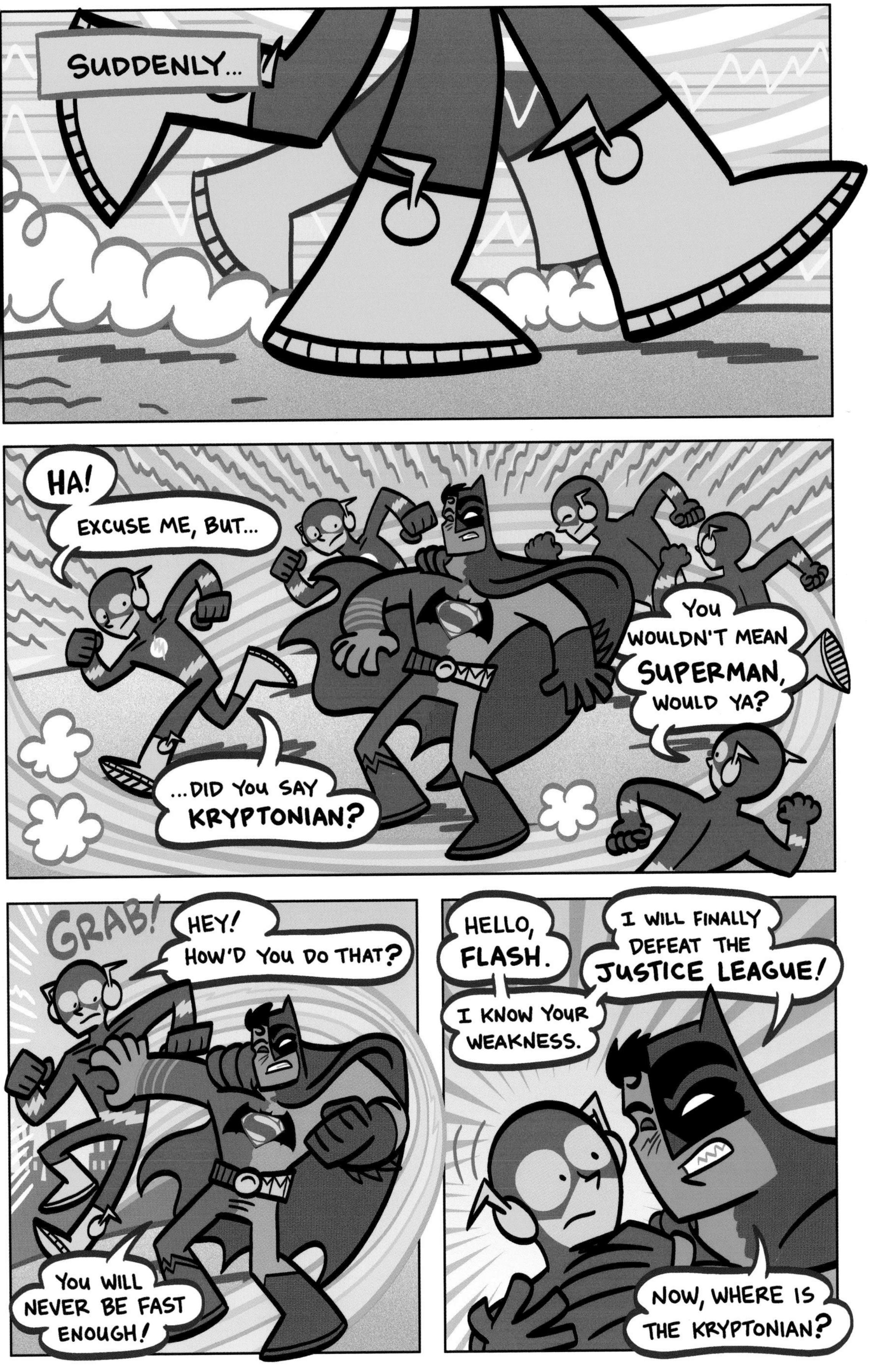
SUDDENLY...
HA!
EXCUSE ME, BUT...
...DID YOU SAY KRYPTONIAN?
YOU WOULDN'T MEAN SUPERMAN, WOULD YA?
GRAB!
HEY! HOW'D YOU DO THAT?
YOU WILL NEVER BE FAST ENOUGH!
HELLO, FLASH.
I KNOW YOUR WEAKNESS.
I WILL FINALLY DEFEAT THE JUSTICE LEAGUE!
NOW, WHERE IS THE KRYPTONIAN?

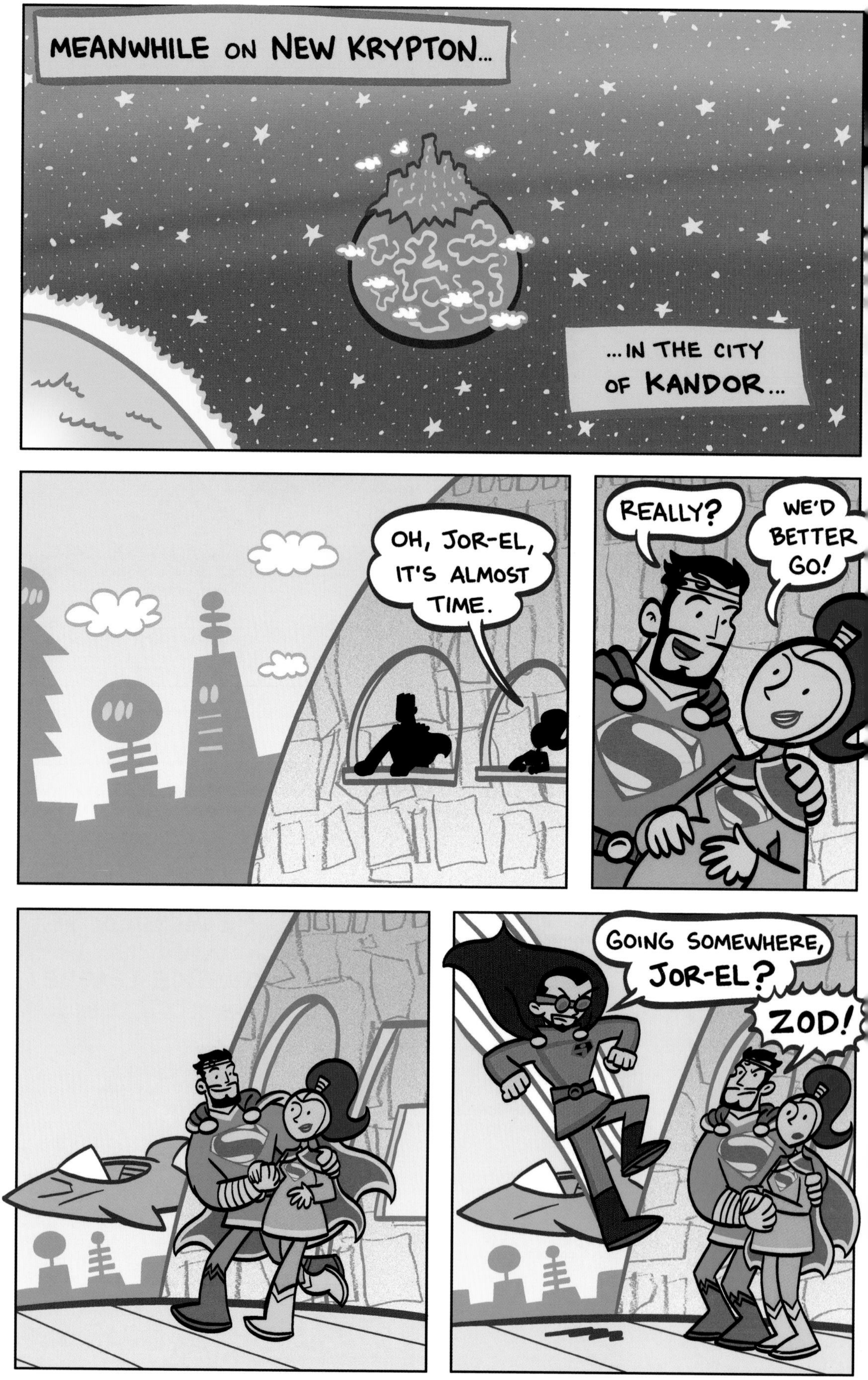
MEANWHILE ON NEW KRYPTON...
...IN THE CITY OF KANDOR...
OH, JOR-EL, IT'S ALMOST TIME.
REALLY?
WE'D BETTER GO!
GOING SOMEWHERE, JOR-EL?
ZOD!

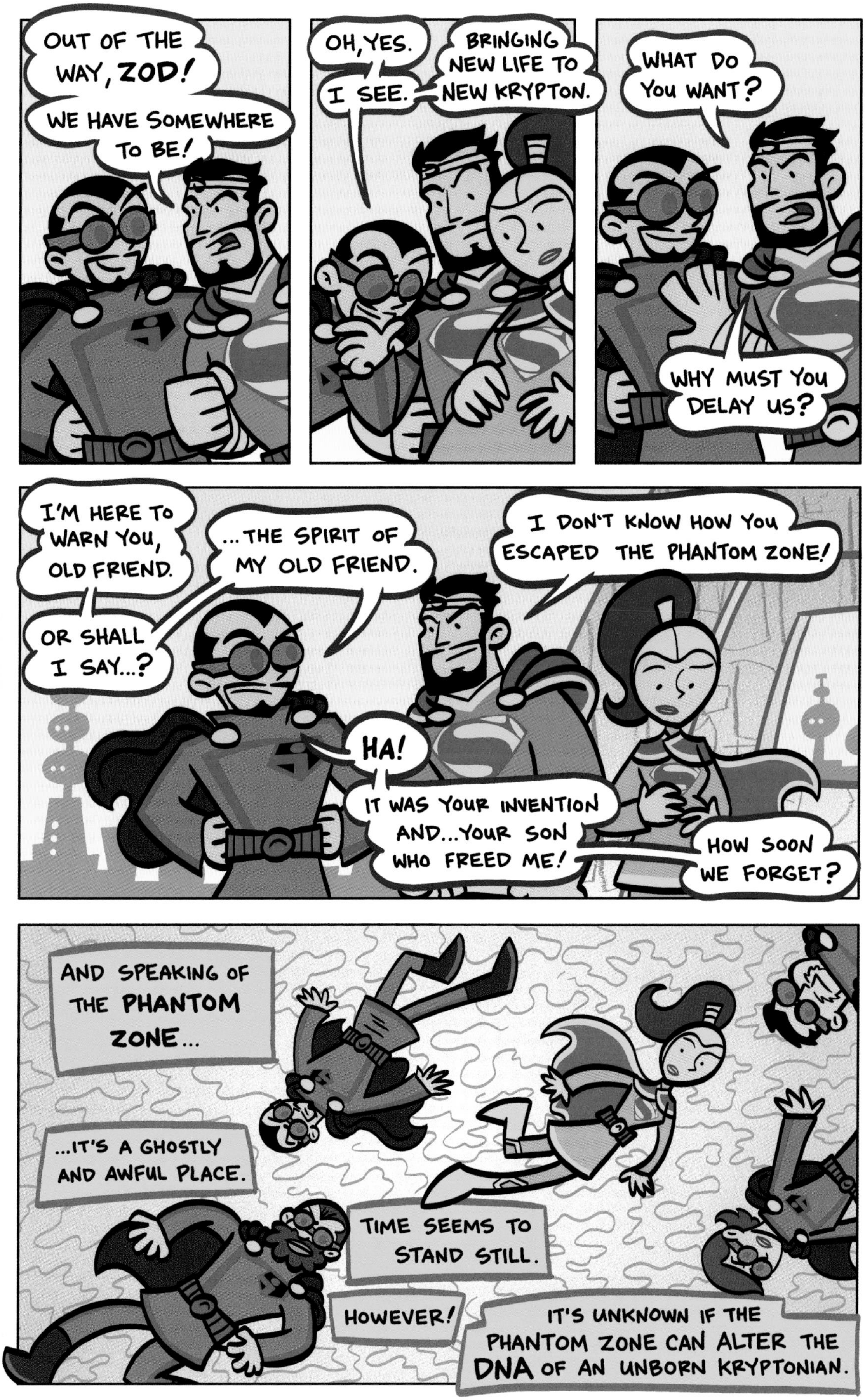
OUT OF THE WAY, ZOD!
WE HAVE SOMEWHERE TO BE!
OH, YES.
I SEE.
BRINGING NEW LIFE TO NEW KRYPTON.
WHAT DO YOU WANT?
WHY MUST YOU DELAY US?
I'M HERE TO WARN YOU, OLD FRIEND.
OR SHALL I SAY...?
...THE SPIRIT OF MY OLD FRIEND.
I DON'T KNOW HOW YOU ESCAPED THE PHANTOM ZONE!
HA!
IT WAS YOUR INVENTION AND...YOUR SON WHO FREED ME!
HOW SOON WE FORGET?
AND SPEAKING OF THE PHANTOM ZONE...
...IT'S A GHOSTLY AND AWFUL PLACE.
TIME SEEMS TO STAND STILL.
HOWEVER!
IT'S UNKNOWN IF THE PHANTOM ZONE CAN ALTER THE DNA OF AN UNBORN KRYPTONIAN.

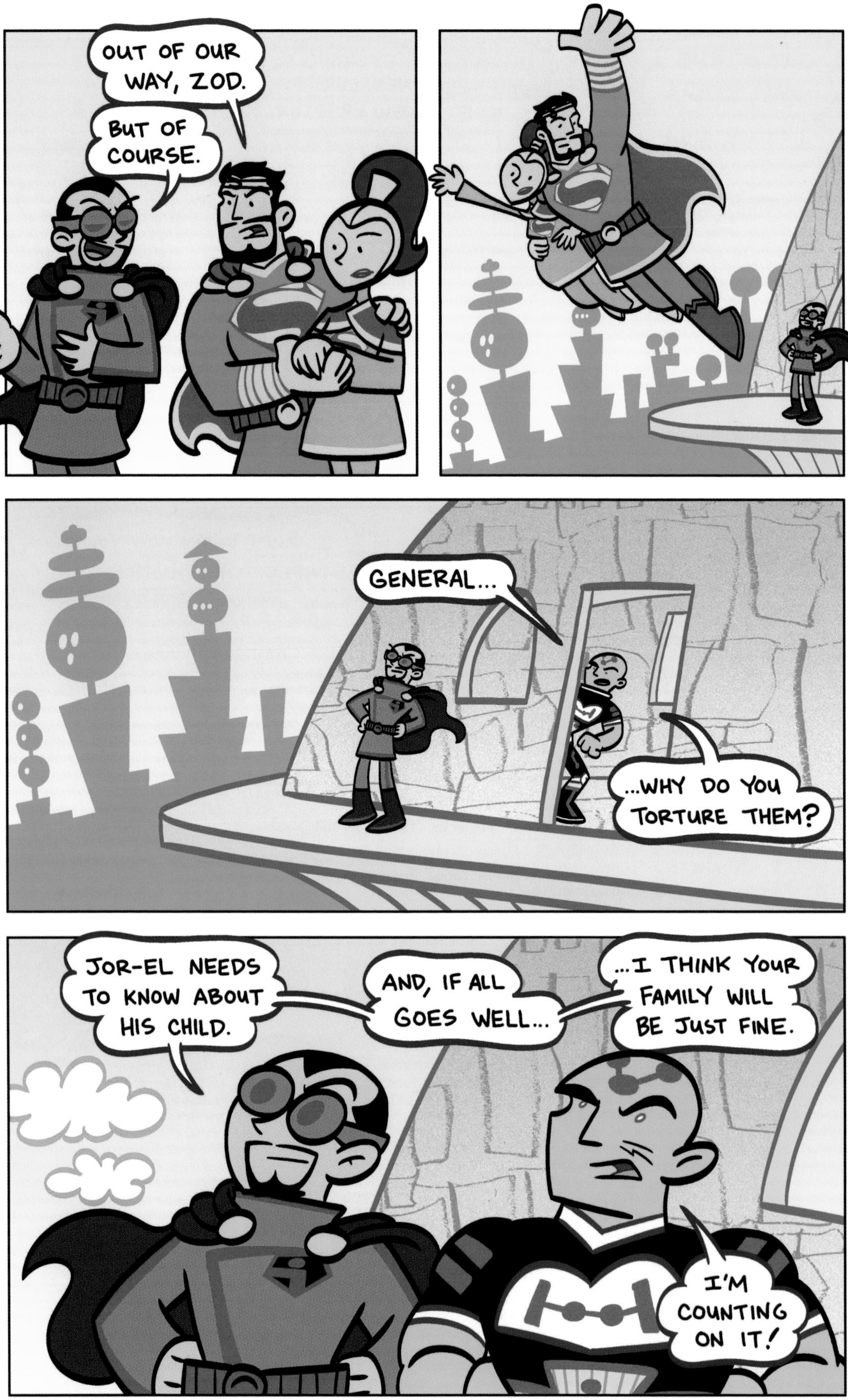
OUT OF OUR WAY, ZOD.
BUT OF COURSE.
GENERAL...
...WHY DO YOU TORTURE THEM?
JOR-EL NEEDS TO KNOW ABOUT HIS CHILD.
AND, IF ALL GOES WELL...
...I THINK YOUR FAMILY WILL BE JUST FINE.
I'M COUNTING ON IT!

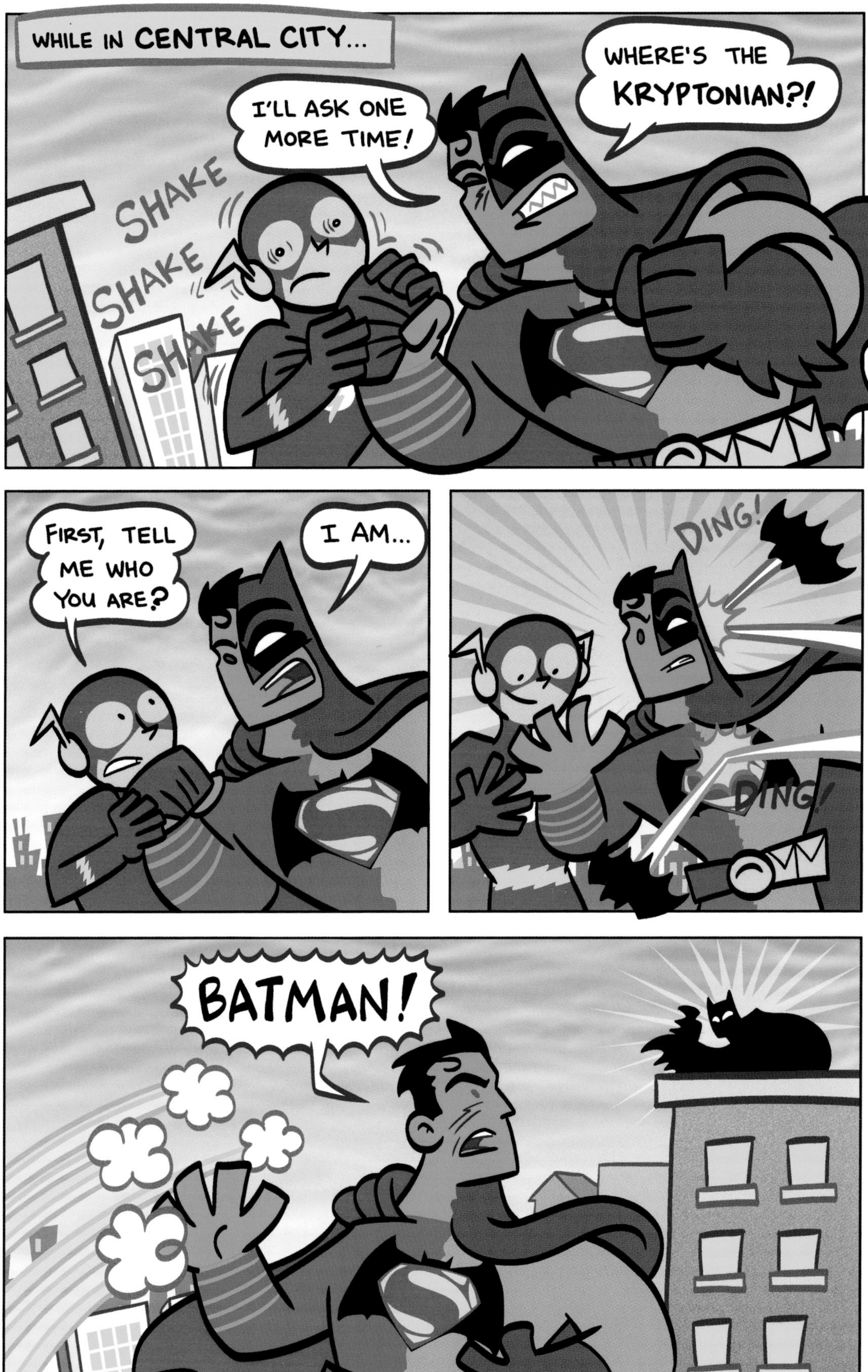
WHILE IN CENTRAL CITY...
I'LL ASK ONE MORE TIME!
WHERE'S THE KRYPTONIAN?!
SHAKE
SHAKE
SHAKE
FIRST, TELL ME WHO YOU ARE?
I AM...
DING!
DING!
BATMAN!

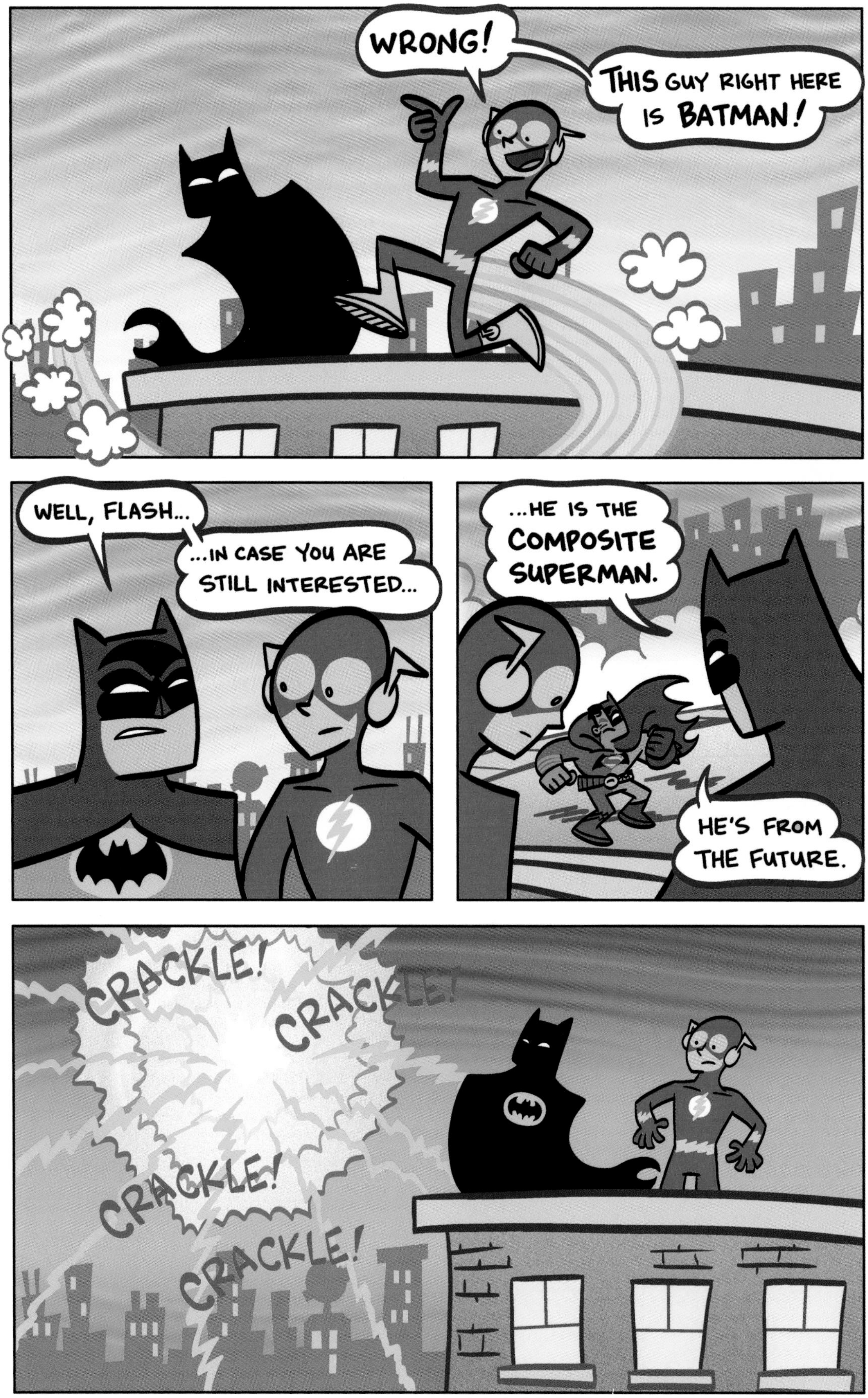

WRONG!
THIS GUY RIGHT HERE IS BATMAN!
WELL, FLASH...
...IN CASE YOU ARE STILL INTERESTED...
...HE IS THE COMPOSITE SUPERMAN.
HE'S FROM THE FUTURE.
CRACKLE!
CRACKLE!
CRACKLE!
CRACKLE!

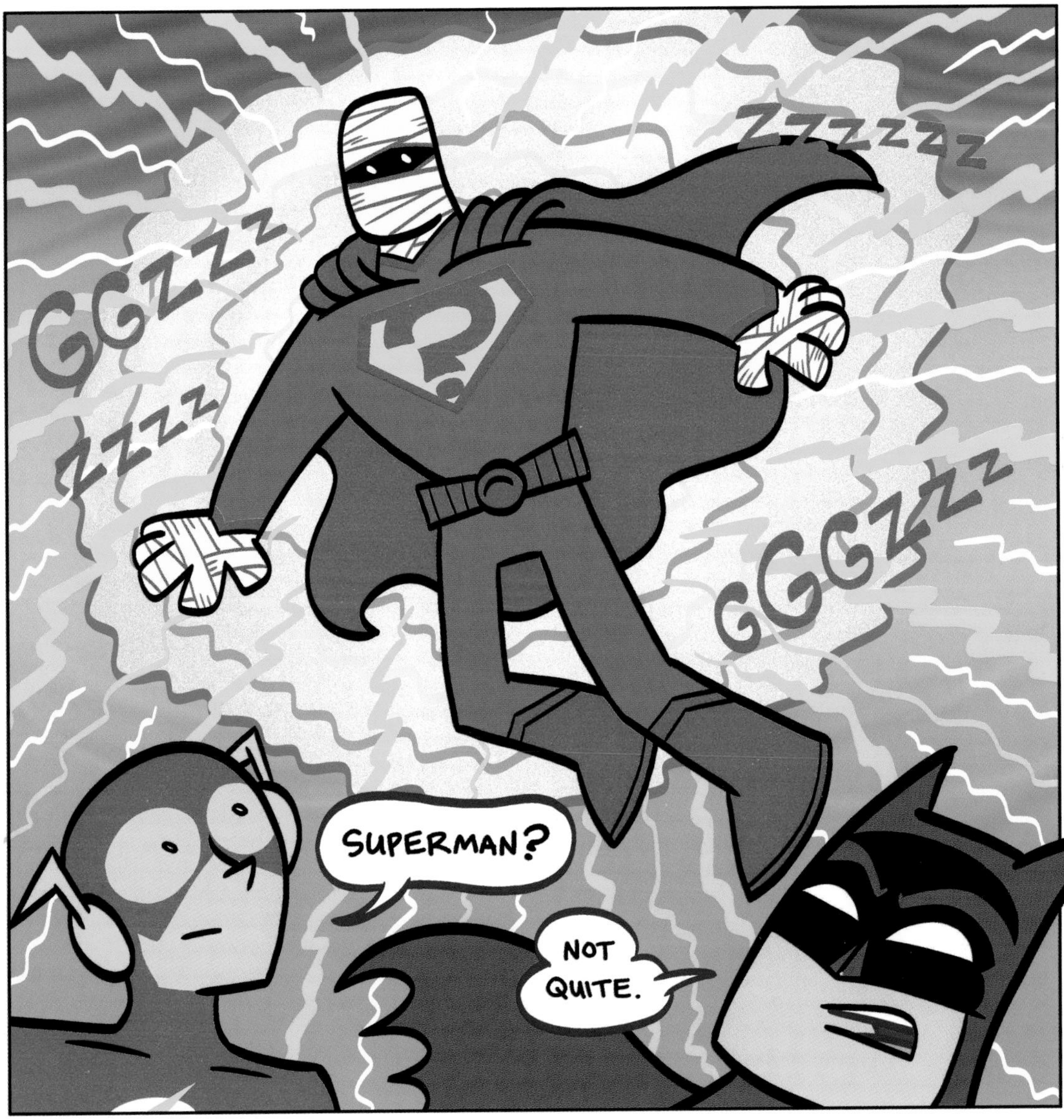
GGZZZZ
ZZZZZ
ZZZZZZZ
GGGZZZZ
SUPERMAN?
NOT QUITE.

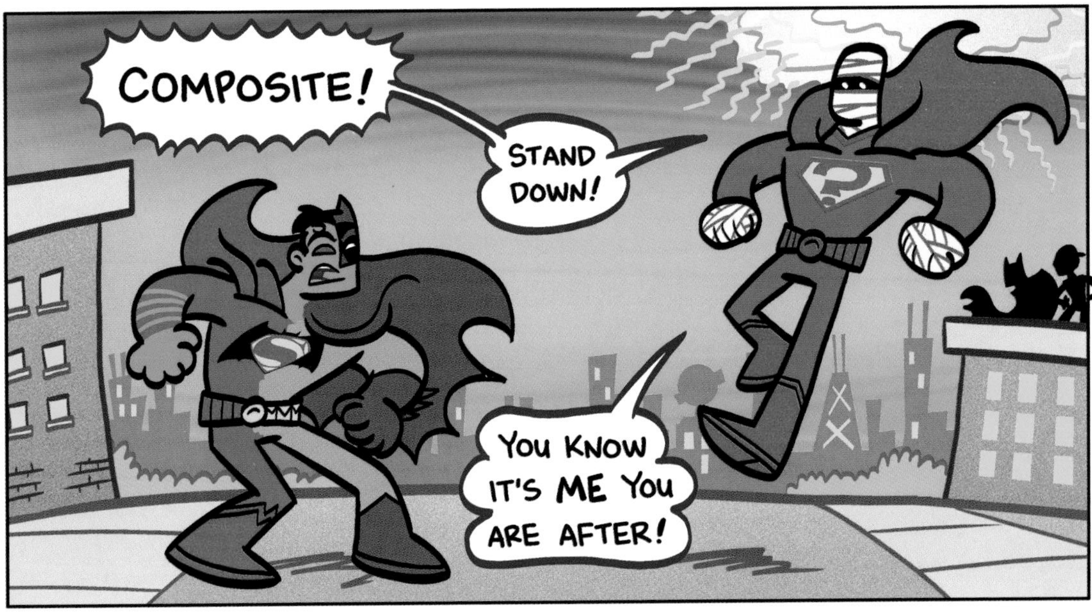
COMPOSITE!
STAND DOWN!
YOU KNOW IT'S ME YOU ARE AFTER!

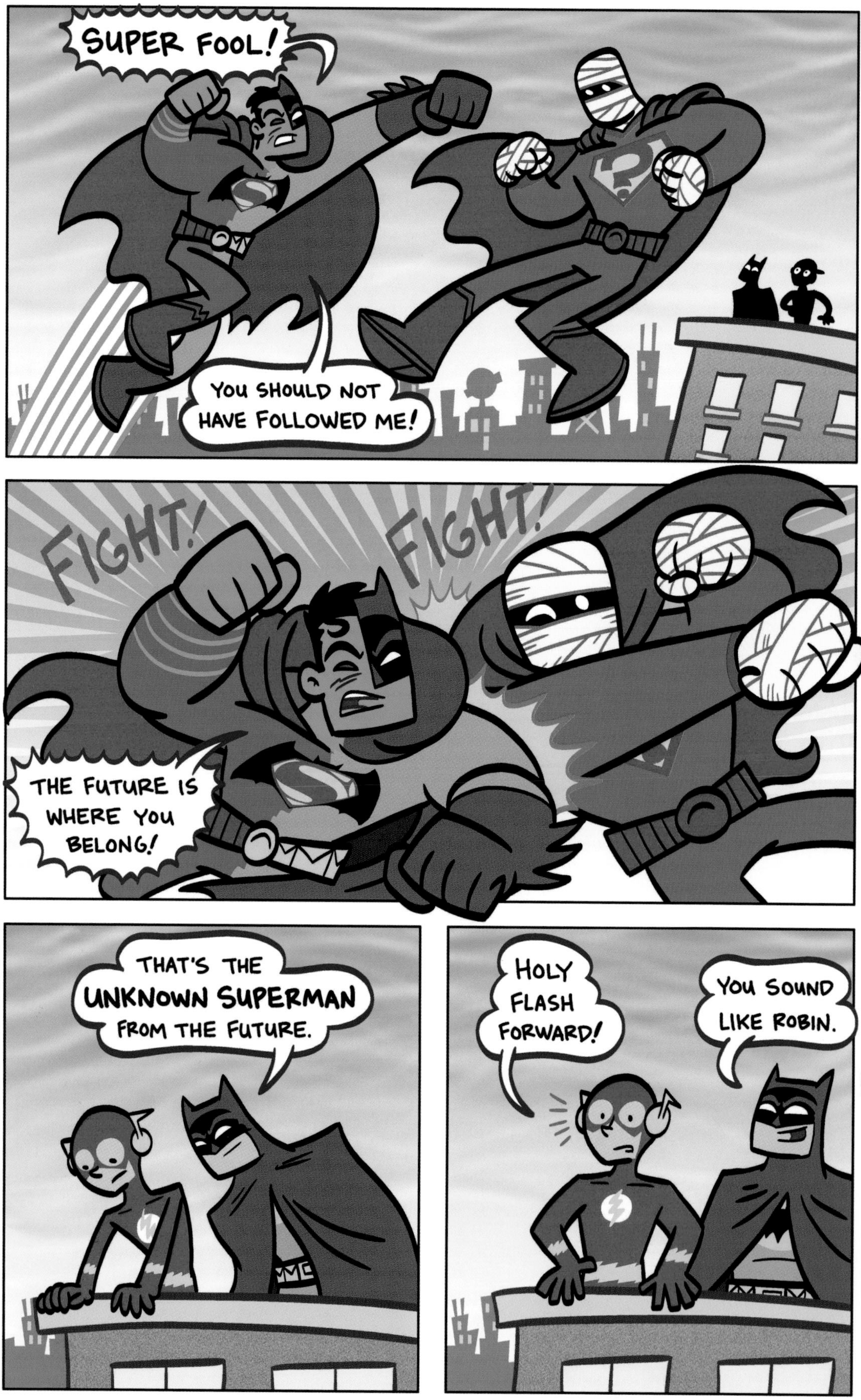
SUPER FOOL!
YOU SHOULD NOT HAVE FOLLOWED ME!
FIGHT! FIGHT!
THE FUTURE IS WHERE YOU BELONG!
THAT'S THE UNKNOWN SUPERMAN FROM THE FUTURE.
HOLY FLASH FORWARD!
YOU SOUND LIKE ROBIN.

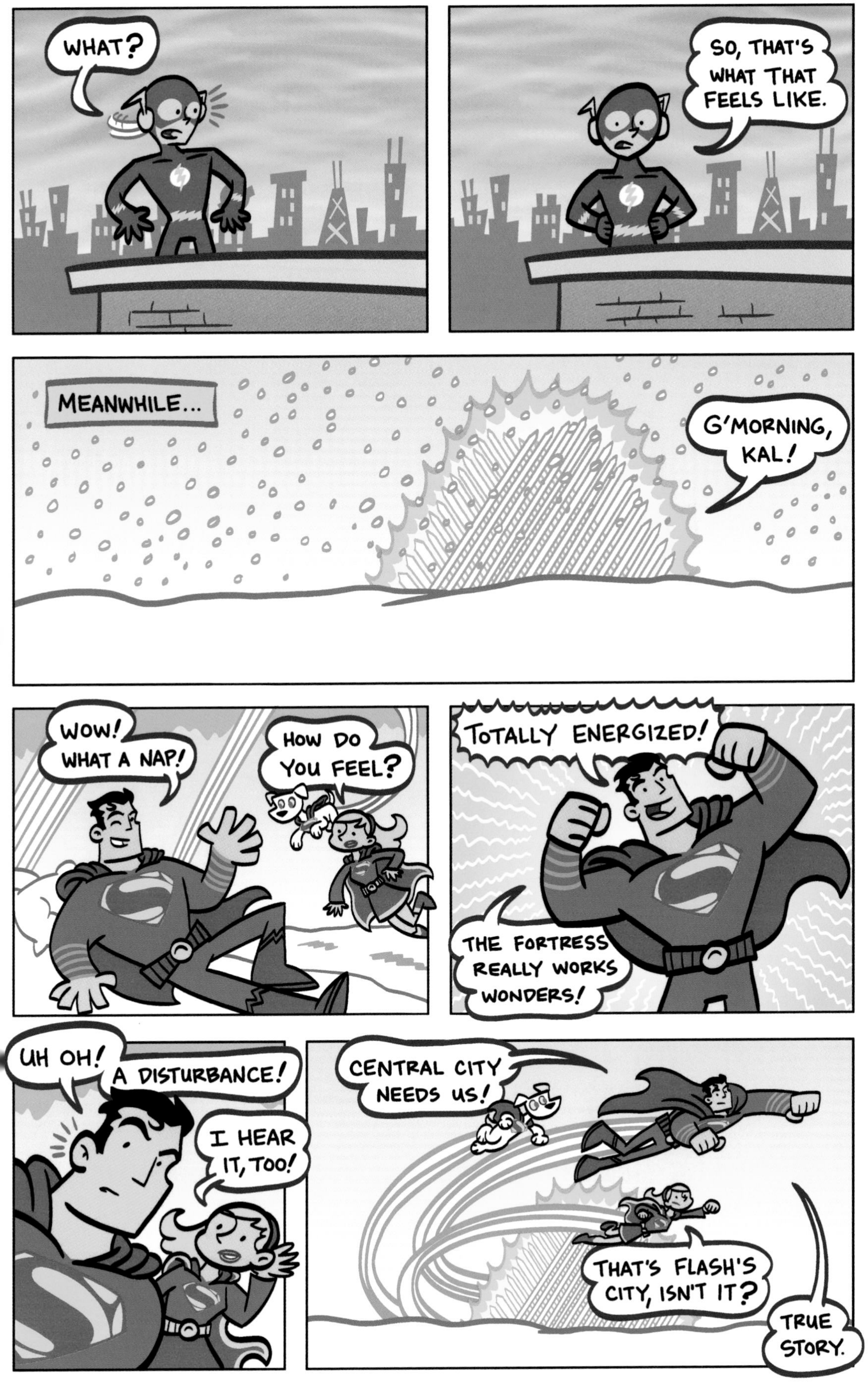
WHAT?
SO, THAT'S WHAT THAT FEELS LIKE.
MEANWHILE...
G'MORNING, KAL!
WOW! WHAT A NAP!
HOW DO YOU FEEL?
TOTALLY ENERGIZED!
THE FORTRESS REALLY WORKS WONDERS!
UH OH!
A DISTURBANCE!
I HEAR IT, TOO!
CENTRAL CITY NEEDS US!
THAT'S FLASH'S CITY, ISN'T IT?
TRUE STORY.

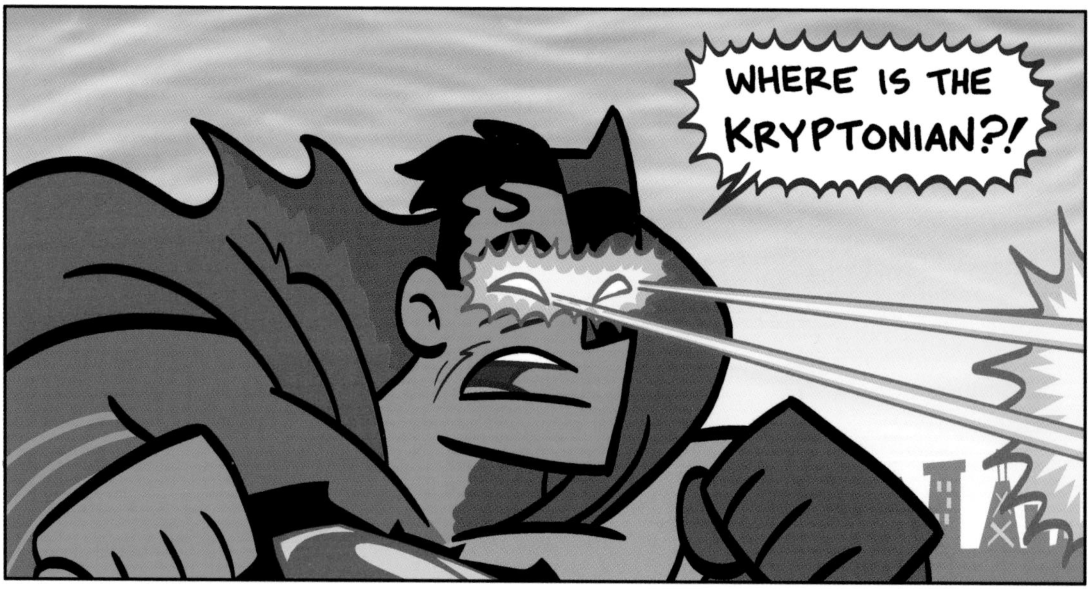
WHERE IS THE KRYPTONIAN?!

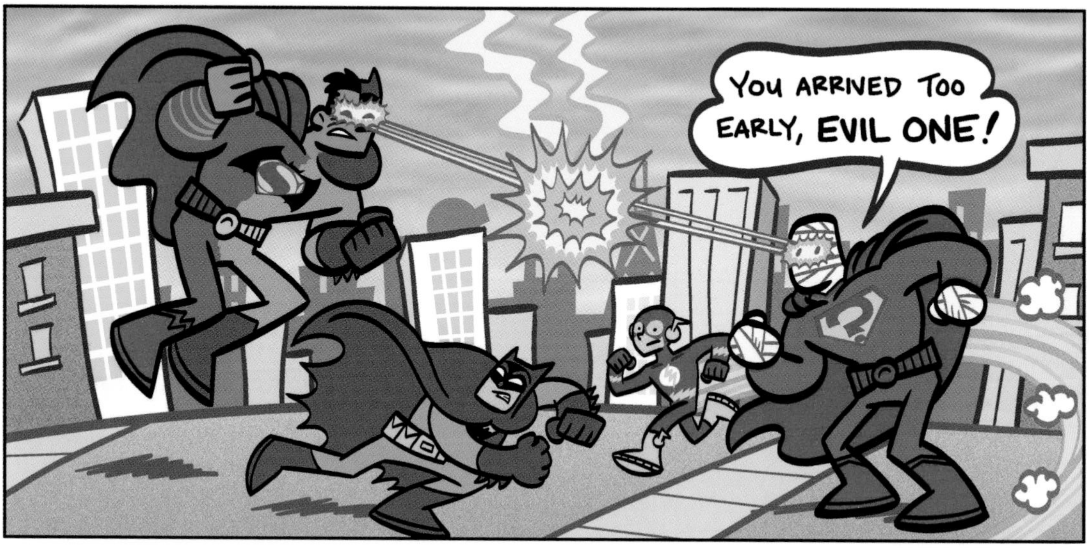
YOU ARRIVED TOO EARLY, EVIL ONE!

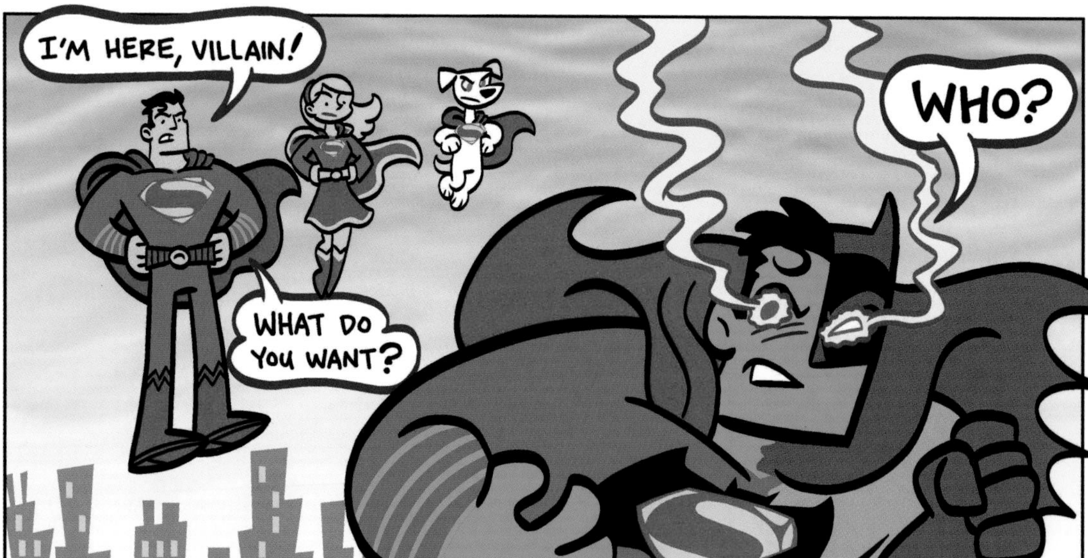
I'M HERE, VILLAIN!
WHAT DO YOU WANT?
WHO?

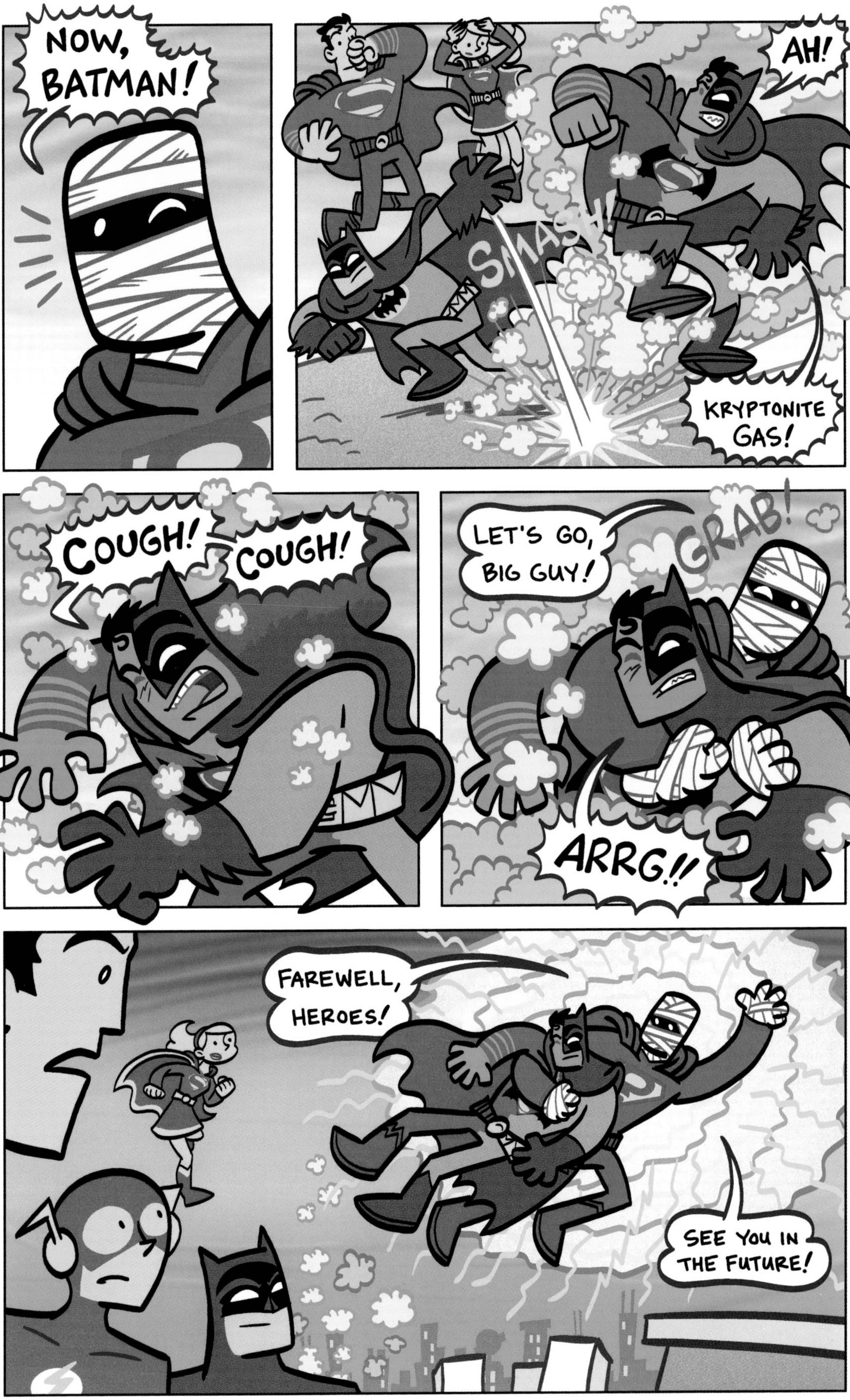
NOW, BATMAN!
AH!
SMASH!
KRYPTONITE GAS!
COUGH! COUGH!
LET'S GO, BIG GUY!
GRAB!
ARRG!!
FAREWELL, HEROES!
SEE YOU IN THE FUTURE!

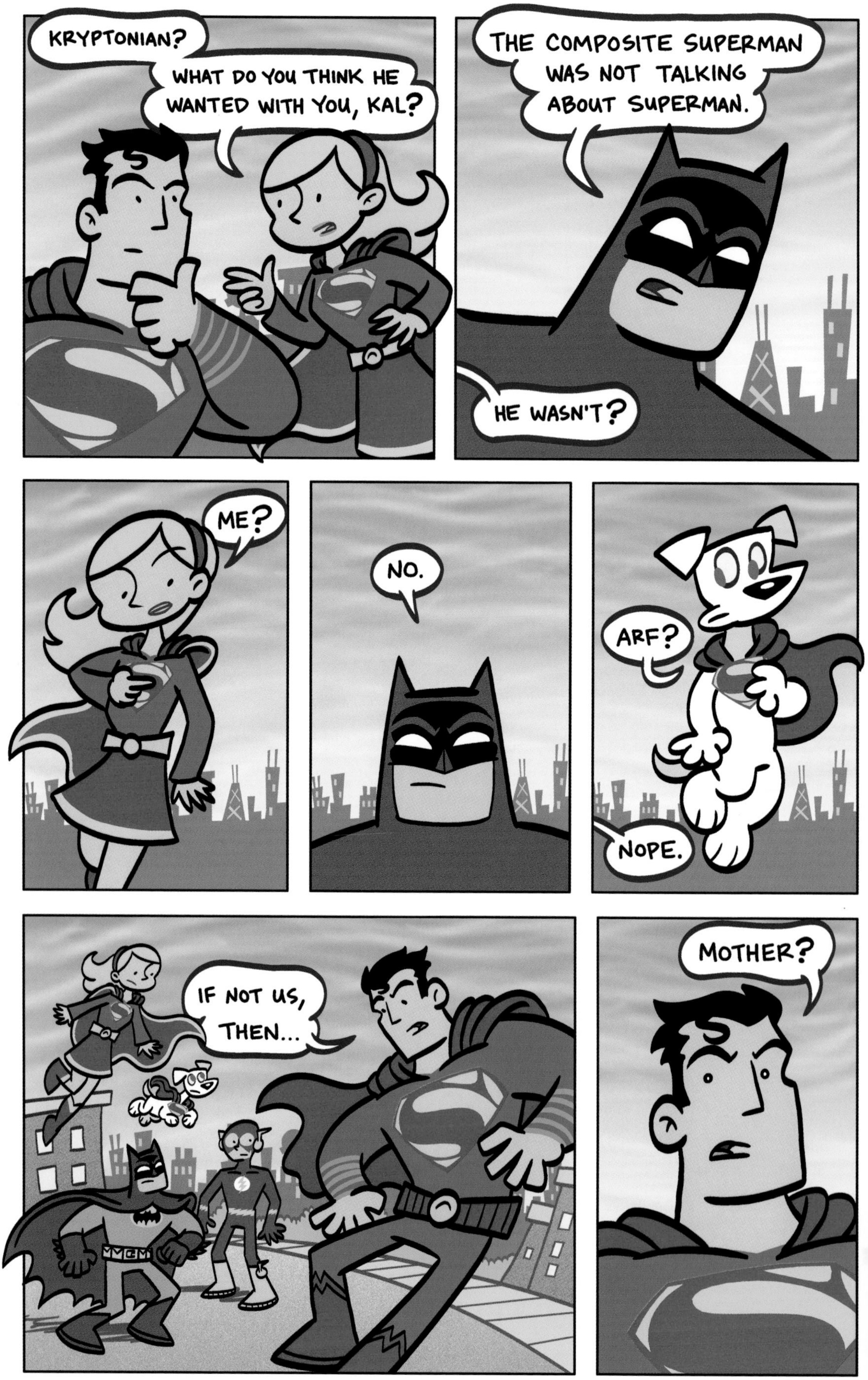
KRYPTONIAN?
WHAT DO YOU THINK HE WANTED WITH YOU, KAL?
THE COMPOSITE SUPERMAN WAS NOT TALKING ABOUT SUPERMAN.
HE WASN'T?
ME?
NO.
ARF?
NOPE.
IF NOT US, THEN...
MOTHER?

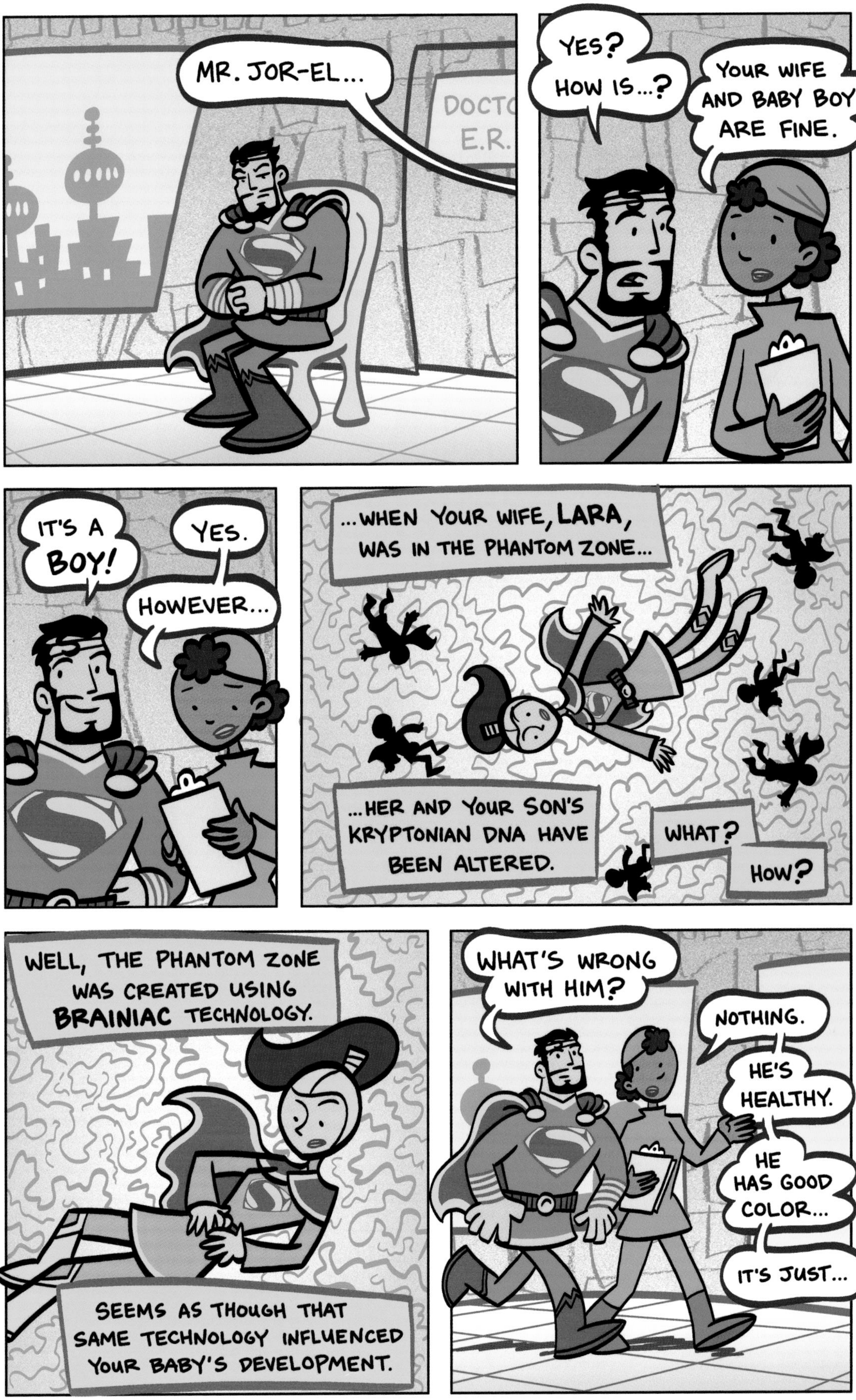

MR. JOR-EL...
DOCTOR E.R.
YES? HOW IS...?
YOUR WIFE AND BABY BOY ARE FINE.
IT'S A BOY!
YES.
HOWEVER...
...WHEN YOUR WIFE, LARA, WAS IN THE PHANTOM ZONE...
...HER AND YOUR SON'S KRYPTONIAN DNA HAVE BEEN ALTERED.
WHAT?
HOW?
WELL, THE PHANTOM ZONE WAS CREATED USING BRAINIAC TECHNOLOGY.
SEEMS AS THOUGH THAT SAME TECHNOLOGY INFLUENCED YOUR BABY'S DEVELOPMENT.
WHAT'S WRONG WITH HIM?
NOTHING.
HE'S HEALTHY.
HE HAS GOOD COLOR...
IT'S JUST...

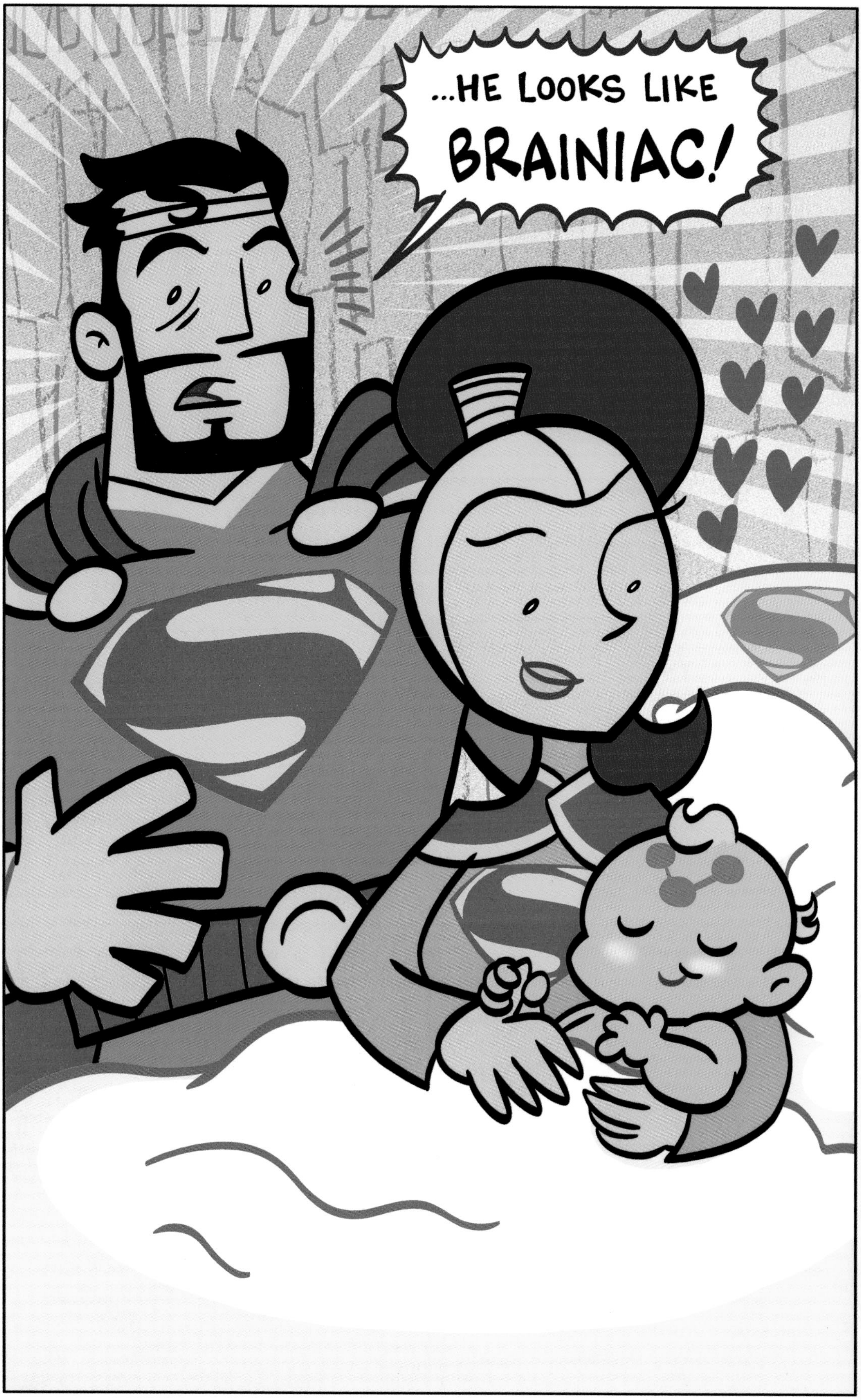
...HE LOOKS LIKE BRAINIAC!

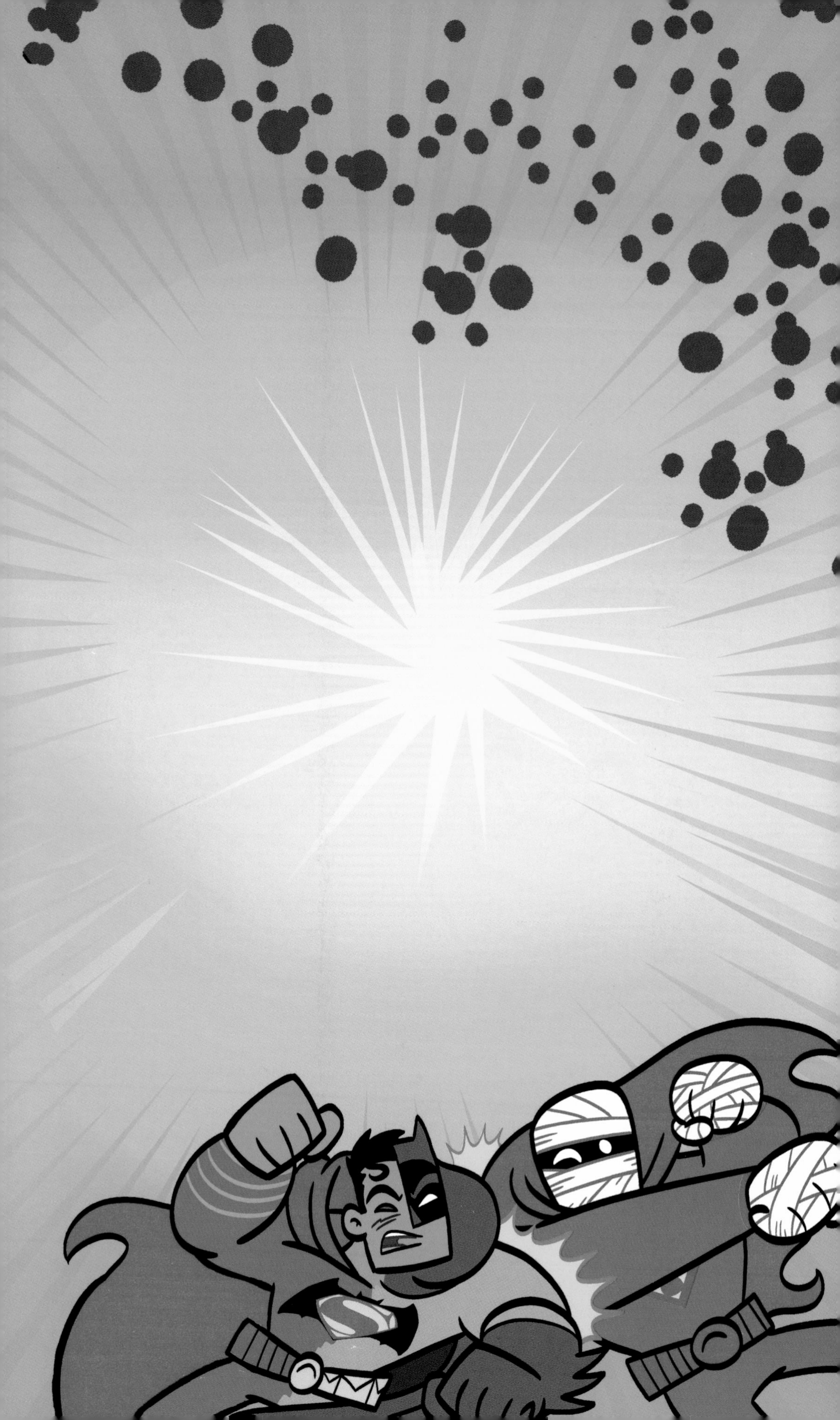

CREATORS

ART BALTAZAR IS A CARTOONIST MACHINE FROM THE HEART OF CHICAGO! HE DEFINES CARTOONS AND COMICS NOT ONLY AS AN ART STYLE, BUT AS A WAY OF LIFE. CURRENTLY, ART IS THE CREATIVE FORCE BEHIND *THE NEW YORK TIMES* BEST-SELLING, EISNER AWARD-WINNING DC COMICS SERIES TINY TITANS, THE CO-WRITER FOR *BILLY BATSON AND THE MAGIC OF SHAZAM!,* AND CO-CREATOR OF SUPERMAN FAMILY ADVENTURES. ART IS LIVING THE DREAM! HE DRAWS COMICS AND NEVER HAS TO LEAVE THE HOUSE. HE LIVES WITH HIS LOVELY WIFE, ROSE, BIG BOY SONNY, LITTLE BOY GORDON, AND LITTLE GIRL AUDREY. RIGHT ON!

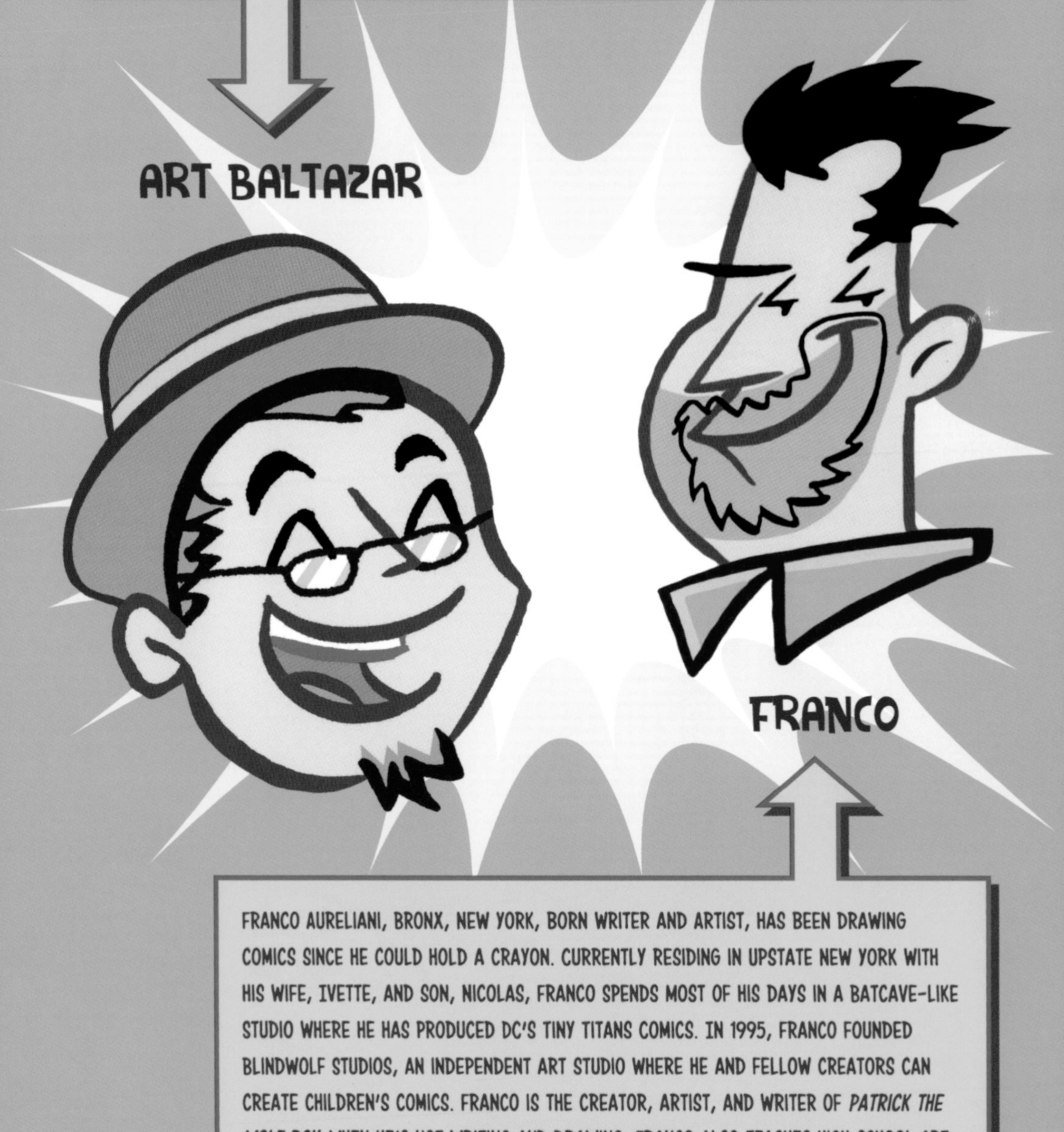
ART BALTAZAR
FRANCO

FRANCO AURELIANI, BRONX, NEW YORK, BORN WRITER AND ARTIST, HAS BEEN DRAWING COMICS SINCE HE COULD HOLD A CRAYON. CURRENTLY RESIDING IN UPSTATE NEW YORK WITH HIS WIFE, IVETTE, AND SON, NICOLAS, FRANCO SPENDS MOST OF HIS DAYS IN A BATCAVE-LIKE STUDIO WHERE HE HAS PRODUCED DC'S TINY TITANS COMICS. IN 1995, FRANCO FOUNDED BLINDWOLF STUDIOS, AN INDEPENDENT ART STUDIO WHERE HE AND FELLOW CREATORS CAN CREATE CHILDREN'S COMICS. FRANCO IS THE CREATOR, ARTIST, AND WRITER OF *PATRICK THE WOLF BOY*. WHEN HE'S NOT WRITING AND DRAWING, FRANCO ALSO TEACHES HIGH SCHOOL ART.

GLOSSARY

commute (kuh-MYOOT)—a long distance to work or school by bus, train, or car

composite (kuhm-PAH-zuht)—made of different parts or elements

delay (di-LAY)—to make someone or something late

disturbance (dis-TURB-ahnts)—an interruption

DNA (dee-en-AY)—material in cells that gives people their individual characteristics; DNA stands for deoxyribonucleic acid

energize (IN-ur-jize)—to fill with fuel, or to give energy

general (JEN-ur-uhl)—the highest rank of an officer in the military

invention (in-VEN-shuhn)—a new idea or machine

nutrient (NOO-tree-uhnt)—a substance needed by a living thing to stay healthy

pathetic (puh-THET-ik)—useless or weak

peasant (PEZ-uhnt)—a common person

portal (POHR-tuhl)—a large door or path between dimensions, worlds, or realms

primitive (PRIM-uh-tiv)—something in its early stage of development

replenish (ri-PLEN-ish)—to make full again

VISUAL QUESTIONS AND WRITING PROMPTS

1. BEATING SUPERMAN IS VERY IMPORTANT TO LEX LUTHOR. WHY DO YOU THINK THAT IS?

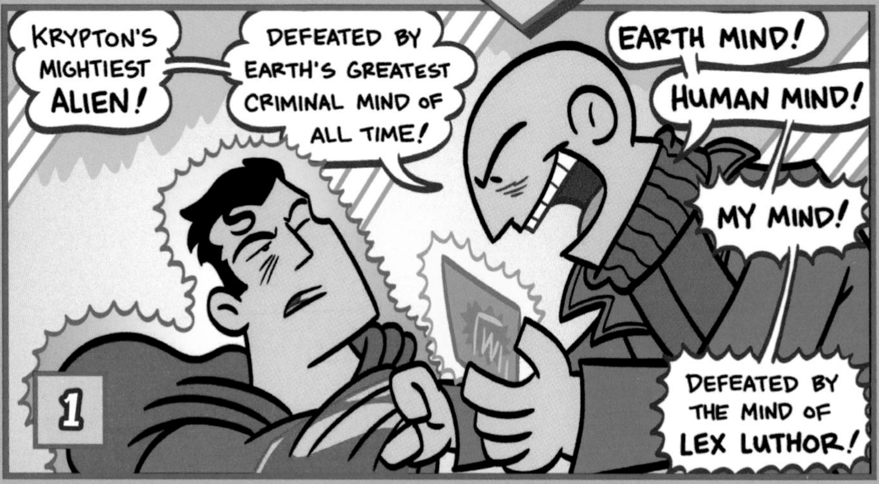

1
KRYPTON'S MIGHTIEST ALIEN!
DEFEATED BY EARTH'S GREATEST CRIMINAL MIND OF ALL TIME!
EARTH MIND!
HUMAN MIND!
MY MIND!
DEFEATED BY THE MIND OF LEX LUTHOR!

2. LOOK AT THE DEFINITION FOR "COMPOSITE" IN THE GLOSSARY. WHY DO YOU THINK THE VILLAIN BELOW IS CALLED COMPOSITE SUPERMAN?

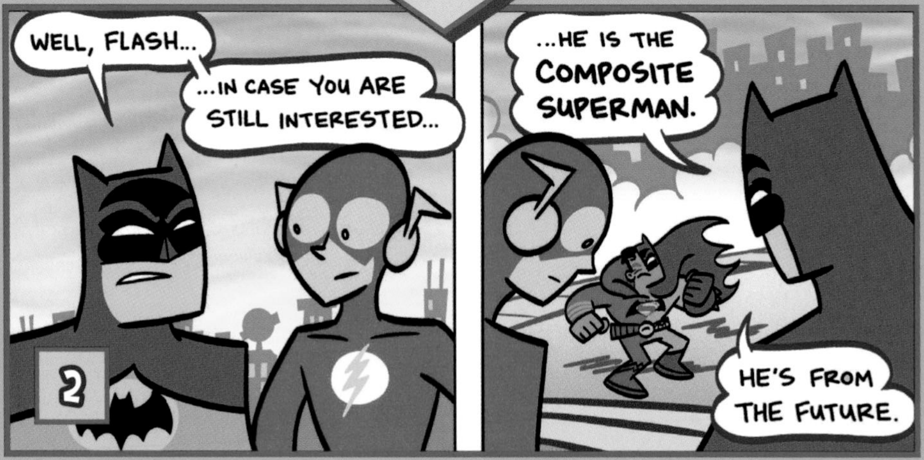

2
WELL, FLASH...
...IN CASE YOU ARE STILL INTERESTED...
...HE IS THE COMPOSITE SUPERMAN.
HE'S FROM THE FUTURE.

3. COMPOSITE SUPERMAN AND UNKNOWN SUPERMAN HAVE FOUGHT EACH OTHER IN THE FUTURE. WRITE ABOUT ONE OF THEIR BATTLES.

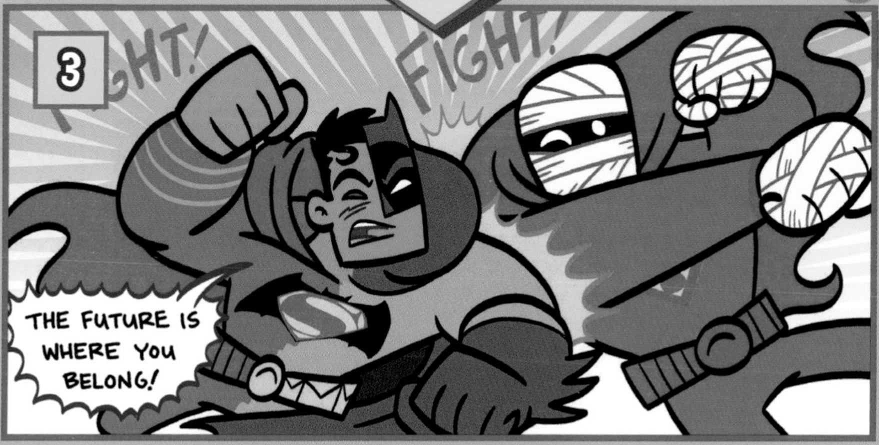
3
FIGHT!
THE FUTURE IS WHERE YOU BELONG!

4. LOOK AT THE DIFFERENCE IN FACIAL EXPRESSIONS BETWEEN JOR-EL AND LARA. WHAT DOES THIS TELL US ABOUT THEIR OPINIONS ON THEIR NEW BABY?

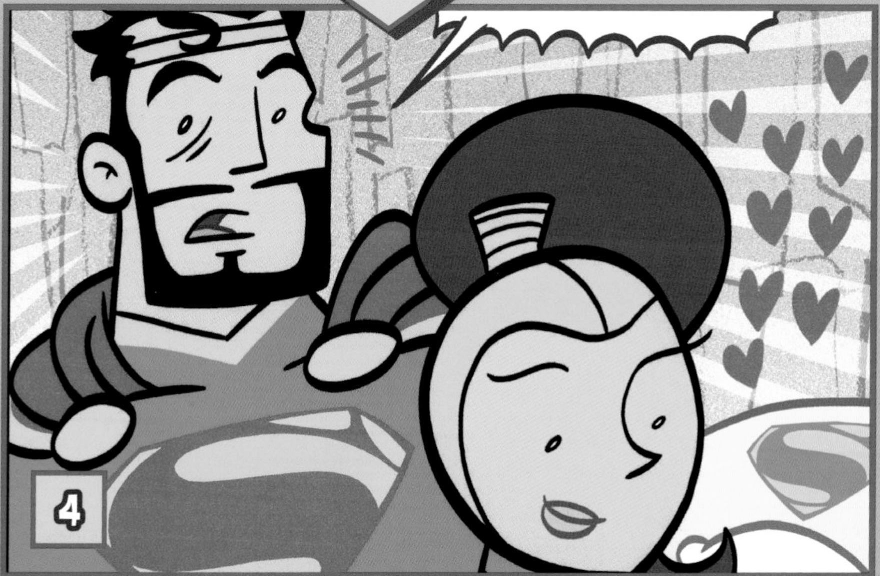
4

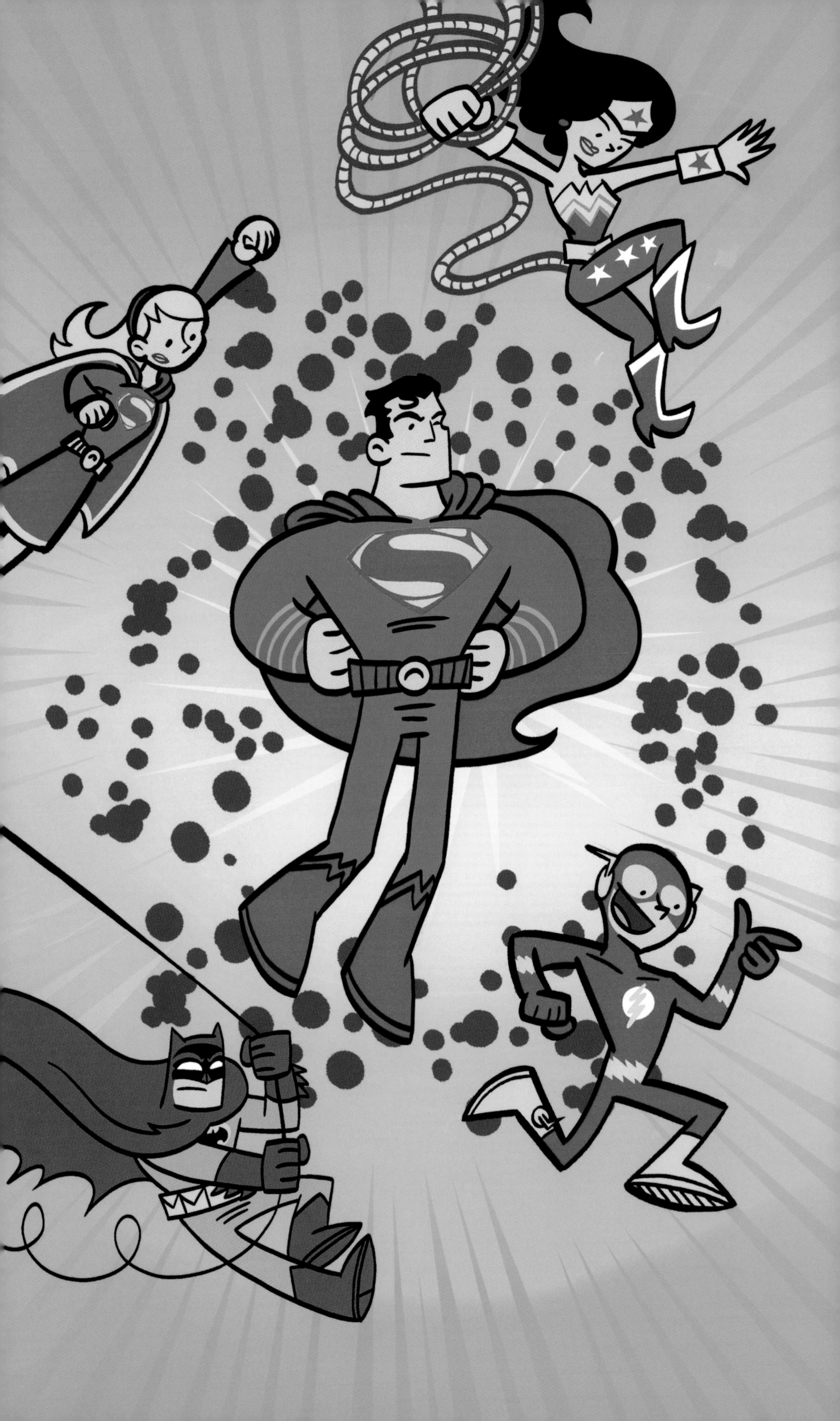

READ THEM ALL!

SUPER POWERS!
Dark Knight Dilemma!
SUPER POWERS!
Composite Crisis!
SUPER POWERS!
Brimstone Attacks!
SUPER POWERS!
League vs Legion!
SUPER POWERS!
Pryme Time!
SUPER POWERS!
The Wrath of Apokolips!

only from

STONE ARCH BOOKS

a capstone imprint

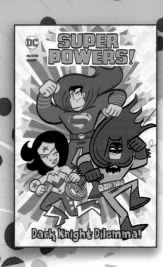

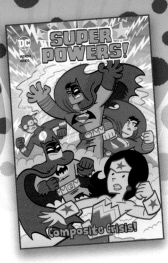

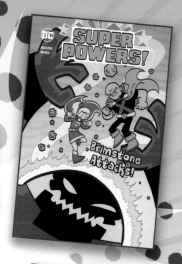

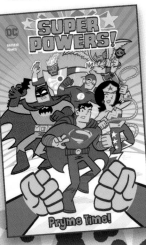

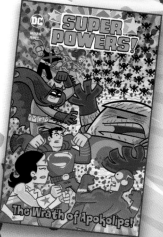

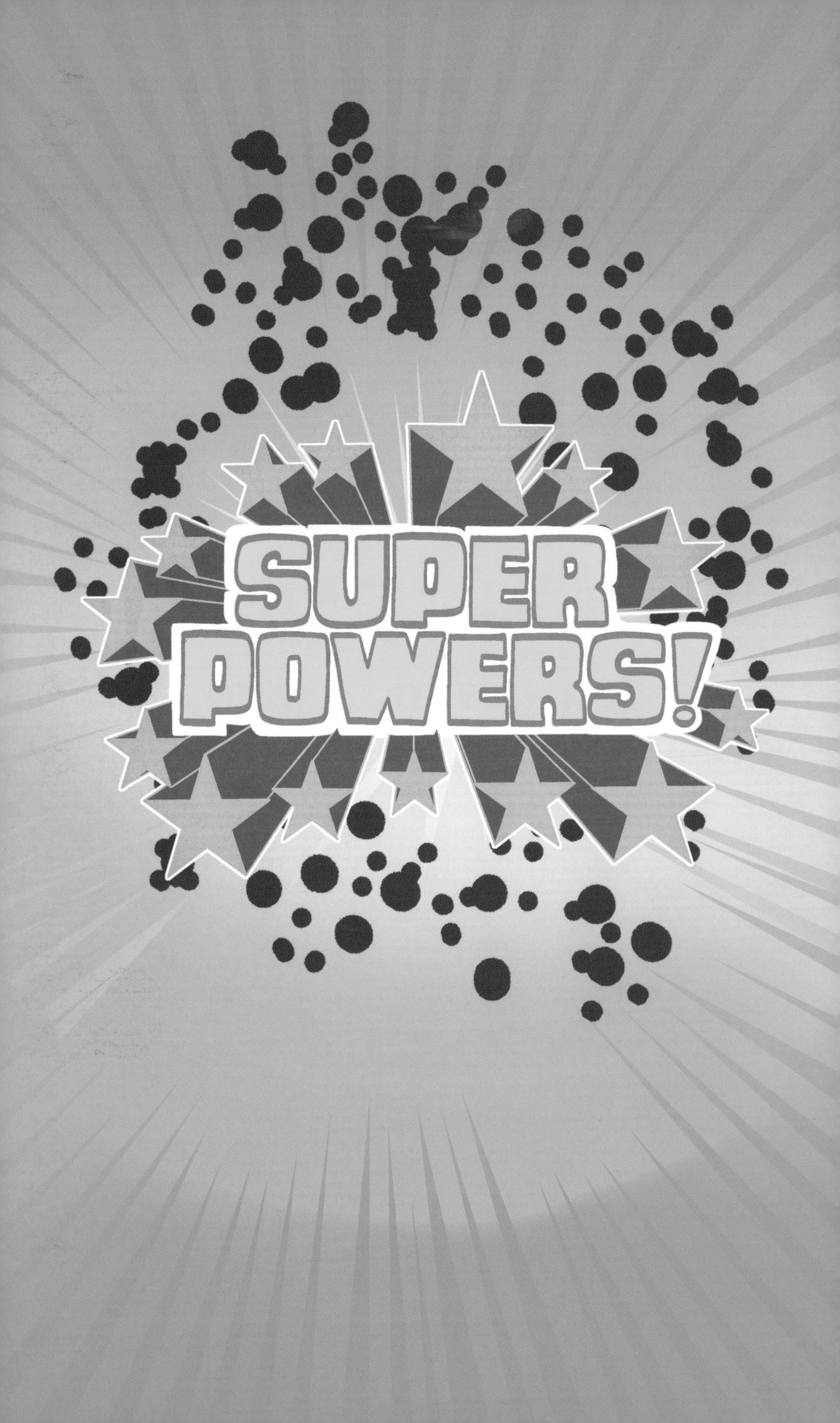
SUPER
POWERS!